MW00899506

THE CONTROL GROUP

e.c. static

Copyright © 2018 E.C. Static

All rights reserved.

ISBN: 9781980544302

CHAPTER ONE

Eris walked home with her eyes turned down, like she always did.

After twenty long years of life, she still couldn't get used to the stares. Everywhere she went, it seemed strangers stared at her until she raised her eyes to theirs, and then they looked away again.

She learned to make herself small. Hid behind beanies and headphones and huge coats. But nothing could hide the emptiness over her head.

That was strange. Irredeemably.

Unrepeatably. Where you could tell anyone else's name and basic physical statistics at a glance, Eris had nothing. She grew up staring at her peers and the magical little boxes of lights hovering over their heads. Became quickly used to the question, "Where are your stats? Are you from somewhere faraway?"

And she would answer, "I'm from *here*," exasperated, embarrassed. The cryptic talk baffled her. Her strangeness walled her in on all sides, blocked her off in a way from everybody. Even her own family looked at her as if she was not fully one of them.

These days, Eris spoke little. She walked to work where she washed dishes alone in a dark room. Walked home again. She was alone, which she liked, because no one stared at the space over her head in disdain or confusion.

She had taken to walking home with music blaring in her ears, her eyes trained on the road.

It was easier to ignore the things people said than to try to forget them later.

It was a little lucky, in retrospect.

She never would have heard him if she did not pause to change the song right then. But then beyond her headphones she heard someone speak. She turned her head and yanked her earphones down.

A homeless man, his face worn by exhaustion and time, sat on a dusty sleeping bag. His stare rooted her to the spot; his eyes were bluer than any she had ever seen. He had hung a piece of tarp over his nest like a roof. Before him sat a tin cup with a couple of one dollar bills.

Eris's dark eyes went wide and dewy with shock. "I'm sorry," she said. "What did you say?"

"I said," the man said, with a tone of lazy surprise, "you're real, too."

She stopped, rooted to the spot. Stared at him directly now.

Just like her, there was no box hovering over his head. He simply sat on the pavement. Existing. Unobtrusive as some piece of the background.

"You don't have a stats bar," she murmured.

"Am I your first one?" His tone was bitter but delighted. "Sit down, pretty girl. Talk with me for a minute. No one ever talks to me anymore."

She sat on the concrete beside him. Breathed through her mouth, discreetly. "What do you mean I'm real?"

"Those other people—" he gestured to the city beyond, the cars whisking past them in a constant ebb and flow "—are not real. You and I are." He smiled, dreamily, his eyes somewhere distant and faraway. "There were more of us, when I was young. I've heard they've begun to dismantle the whole thing."

Eris could only stare at him. Wondering if

he was mentally ill. If she was an idiot for sitting here listening to him ramble.

But he did not sound ill. He sounded very tired, and very sane.

"What's your name?" she asked him.

"Cassius." His stare probed her face for something. She was not sure what to offer him. "You must be one of the controls."

"I honestly don't know what you're talking about."

That made him start laughing in real joy and delight. He stood up and began gathering up his things. Placed them in a torn but serviceable trash bag.

"You can buy me a coffee," he told Eris, cheerily. "And I will explain everything."

She gripped her headphones, tightly. Panic chased itself in circles in her belly like a dog after its own tail.

Finally she managed, dizzily, "Okay, then."

CHAPTER TWO

Naturally they garnered stares in the cafe. Eris soothed her anxiety with the fact that this could only be because Cassius was carrying a black garbage bag full of his belongings and glaring around dismissively at everyone.

They ordered two black coffees and sat beside the window. Cassius put his bag delicately beneath his seat, as if anyone here was going to try to steal it.

Eris sank into the chair across from him. Wished she could melt into it. She cupped both hands over the sides of her face and said to him,

"Well, now they're all fucking staring at us."

"Oh, I'll fix that." Cassius cupped his hands around his mouth and called out to the room, "Hey! Stop fucking staring at us!"

And all the eyes turned away.

The old man shrugged. Drank his coffee, even though it was steaming hot. "It's kind of a socially stupid AI, I've learned. You need to be very direct that you don't like something."

Eris moved her hands shakily to her coffee cup. Gripped the warmth. Willed it to ground her. The cafe was spinning like it was its own tiny planet on a strange sideways axis.

Cassius regarded her over the rim of his coffee cup. "How old are you, Eris?"

"Twenty," she said.

"How did you live this long without ever happening upon the truth?"

She did not know how to answer that, so she only said, "I have no idea what you're talking about."

"Do you ever notice that all the little details here just don't... mesh? How your coffee tastes different from one day to the next? Or how you can wake up twice in one morning and not even notice the little glitch?"

Eris sipped her coffee to avoid having to speak. He really was mad. Everyone stopped looking because no one keeps looking at some dirty old man who yelled *hey, stop fucking staring at us!* in a coffee shop.

Her mind raced. Planning an exit. Did the bathroom have a window? Could she ask the barista to call the police?

"Everything you see or touch or taste--" he chuckled, held up the coffee cup for an example. "It's imaginary. A simulation. A very fine one, but all of it little ones and zeroes, in the end."

"My coffee doesn't taste like ones and zeroes," she said, not daring to look up from the table.

Cassius lowered his head. Tried to catch her eye. "You understand, don't you, Eris? You're not the strange one. *They* are. You're a human being purposefully raised in a world of robotic intelligence."

"I don't understand what any of that means. Or why you're even telling me this."

The old man slumped back into his chair. He shrugged. "You deserve to know. There was a small group of you who was never meant to know. The control group. It's necessary, you know, in psychology. Do you know anything about psychology?"

She couldn't help her scoff. "Do *you?*"

That earned a smile. "I think I know a thing or two more than you do, yes. I have devoted my life to researching the people who trapped us here."

"Trapped." Eris pushed her chair away from the table with a loud scrape. "I think you should call a doctor, honestly."

"There is a world out there where you are just like everyone else, and the trees change color and lose their leaves, and people say more than the same seventy things *over and over and over again.*"

Her pulse quickened. She had asked her mother, once, if she noticed that her father always had the same jokes, the same barely contextual responses.

And her mother had just laughed and kissed the top of her head and said as she always did, "That's just your father, dear!"

Eris looked up at the cafe's soft domed lighting. At the people murmuring amongst themselves, pointedly ignoring them now. The barista just stood there at the register, smiling blankly at the door, waiting.

"Ah." Cassius grinned and pointed at her. "I see that look. You're not stupid. You notice the little things."

"I think I should go home." The world seemed tilted and strange. Like she was staring at it through the bottom of a glass bottle. Everyone's face seemed as empty as an old building, every smile vacant and painted.

Uncanny. That was the word. It was real and not real all at once.

Except Cassius, smirking across the table at her. His eyes full of knowing delight.

"Do you know more people like us?" she asked.

"Oh, sure. I could even introduce you, if you wanted."

Eris couldn't stop herself from saying yes.

CHAPTER THREE

Three days later, she met Cassius late in the evening in a part of the city she had barely ever visited. They were on the east side, beyond the river, where the buildings were old and slumping. So old that they were from the age that still used things like wood and stone to make buildings.

The address Cassius gave her brought her to an unmarked black door between a barber shop and a pawn shop with heavy bars on its windows.

She rang the doorbell. The air was cool and

tasted like spring. The wind tugged gently at the leaves. Cassius had said the leaves change colors in the real world. It occurred to her for the first time that there was a season other than spring.

The door opened.

Cassius had found somewhere to sleep recently, apparently. His hair looked clean, his clothes fresh. He shook Eris's hand warmly when he saw her.

"I'm glad you've decided to come. We usually meet every other Thursday, but I asked them to make an exception and do a repeat week."

"Why?"

"To meet you."

Blood collected hotly in her ears and cheeks. "Well, shit. Now I feel weird. You didn't have to do that."

He shook his head and hustled her inside. The door opened up into a small stairwell with mailboxes and a laundry room the size of a broom closet. Cassius nodded up the rickety stairs.

"Graham's place is just up there."

The many rows of apartments and doors were crooked and worn. The whole building smelled faintly wet, like mildew and rot. It was a marvel it hadn't been torn down yet.

But the apartment Cassius led her to seemed homey enough. Art on the walls and warm yellow light. The furniture was patched and mismatched, but everything smelled like lavender. Candles burned on every surface in place of electric light.

And the three people sitting before her had nothing over their heads.

Eris shut the door behind her. Stared in wonder and thrill that was horror and joy all at once. She looked to Cassius, nervously.

"Don't be shy. I'll introduce you."

So Eris followed him into the apartment. Two men and a woman sat scattered on the couch and two armchairs. They greeted Eris and Cassius with a host of scattered hellos.

One of them rose to get a dining room chair for Cassius.

"Thank you, Graham," he said and settled into it with a weary sigh.

Eris sat in the only empty armchair. She watched the line of Graham's back as he returned to his seat. He was tall, large-shouldered. He had a look to him of constant muted worry. His hair was dark, curly, meticulous.

When Graham looked toward her, she snapped her stare down at her knees.

Cassius introduced them in turn.

Graham: the brown eyes that made her want to stare a little too long.

Malia: fierce. Sat with her heavy construction boots on the table and appraised Eris, her face twisted with mistrust.

Leo: pale and near-silent. He looked as

anxious as Eris felt. Some part of her wanted to unwind and laugh with him, *god, aren't people just so fucking scary?*

But her throat clamped tightly shut and she could only sit there, surveying the floor, feeling utterly watched.

"Eris," Cassius continued, voice lilting and delighted, "is one of the controls."

That drew raised eyebrows from all three.

Malia smirked. She had black hair, long and thick and curly. She twirled it into a bun as she spoke. "Then you have no clue what's going on."

"I've given her an extremely rough crash course."

"Exactly what we'd expect from you." Graham pulled his slender phone out of his pocket and checked the time. "Why couldn't all this have waited until next week, Cassius?"

"Because she is our way out."

The other three stared at him in mixed

states of perplexion and scorn.

"I think you need to explain a few more steps of that thought process." Malia's voice was cheery but toothed. She was small but muscled and sat like she was used to being the last word in the room.

Graham, who sat on the end of the couch nearest Eris's chair, leaned over the arm to ask her quietly, "Could I get you anything to drink? Some tea or coffee or anything?"

"No, um. I'm good."

"Sorry those two are *so* intense." He smiled. The air between them felt warm and full of new little secrets. "They are mostly benign, despite appearances."

Eris permitted a tiny smile. "Really?"

Cassius prattled on, oblivious to them, "She is our poster child. We stick to the original plan, but she should be the real icon of our cause." He jabbed a finger at Eris. "She's what they're suggesting, after all."

She tried not to feel weirdly guilty.

"Oh my god," Graham said, "you're the rudest person I've ever met. Stop talking about Eris like she's not even here."

"I don't have time to be polite. This is serious!"

Malia gave Eris a smile that was half pity and half teasing. "You have no idea what we're talking about, do you?"

"Of course I don't," Eris muttered, shy despite herself. She should fit right in here. All these people, just as unmarked as she was. But she felt stranger than ever.

"Our world exists to prove a theory." Cassius leaned forward on his elbows and smiled like this was all a fun invented story. "The idea is that human beings can thrive and achieve full self-efficacy even among artificial intelligence. Do you know that word? We talked about psychology, earlier."

Malia rolled her eyes. "This isn't a fucking

lecture, Dr. Nothing."

"Could you try shutting up? That's my favorite thing you do."

Leo glanced between the two of them in alarm.

"If you two can't talk without fighting, I won't let you talk. We've been over this." Graham scowled between Cassius and Malia.

Finally the old man growled, "I apologize," his dark glare matching Malia's.

Then, speaking for the first time, Leo said in a voice soft and clear, "They're trying to test if humans can be raised and live among bots without even noticing it. Or if they can still live fulfilling lives when they *do* realize it. And you're the control group."

"The control group," Eris repeated, numbly.

"They let us know," Malia said, leaning forward, voice dripping bitterness, "to see if we'll go fucking mad or not. And you get to live in perfect ignorance."

"Sure, frame it that way." Cassius groaned. "God, you're such a Debbie Downer all the time."

"Who even *says* that?"

"Plenty of people, when I was your age."

"You're not my age," Malia snapped back.

"Oh, look. You've lost the privilege to talk." Graham clapped his hands together. Cassius started to protest, but Graham just shook his head. "My apartment. My rules."

Eris's anxiety hadn't left her. But it did have a new focus. These people did not frighten her, exactly; the world out there did.

"What are you going to do about it, exactly?" she asked.

CHAPTER FOUR

Graham blinked at her. "About what?"

"About... everything. Cassius just said you have some sort of plan."

Malia barked a laugh. "Plan is a strong word."

Graham shushed her.

"You know what--" Cassius started.

"If you can't respect your silence order until you both calm down, you'll be barred from the apartment for the rest of the evening." That made Malia roll her darkly lined eyes. But she settled back into the couch and gave the old man a needling glare, as if daring him to speak.

Cassius strode out of the room, muttering, and returned with a beer. Graham narrowed his eyes at that but said nothing.

Eris looked between the two most well-hinged people in the room. "What is it all of you do, anyway?"

"We really just get together and bitch," Graham said.

All four of them started laughing at that. Eris's grin was instant and easy for once. She hid it the moment she caught herself doing it.

Leo elaborated, "There's little else we can do. We're more or less just digitized consciousnesses, put in this tiny world. The universe stops forty miles outside the city. I know you haven't tried to go out that far." Color rushed to Eris's cheeks. "It's fine. Don't feel bad. They literally program you to lack the initiative for that."

"Program me," she repeated, her throat thick with tears or vomit. She couldn't tell which yet. "But you said I'm real."

"You are. But here they set the parameters on reality. And if they want to make you oblivious to certain thoughts, they can." Leo shrugged. His smile was small and foxlike. "Until certain people point them out to you directly, of course."

The old man sipped his beer slowly. Watched the wall like he was trying to pick it apart with his eyes.

"Our sort of, like..." Graham waved his hand, vaguely. "Ideal goal is to get the people who run the experiment to realize that this isn't livable." He paused, then reached out and squeezed Eris's knee. "Oh. God. You still don't know what all of this is for."

Eris shifted away from his hand and glanced between them all. Everyone's looks had soured, gone serious and grey. "I don't even really know what you mean."

Graham sighed. "Alright, old man. We need your history lesson. You may speak if you refrain from antagonizing."

Cassius scoffed into his beer. "How very noble of you." He pulled his back up straighter in his chair and popped his neck, loudly. "I'm part of the first round. It's rare to see an old-timer like me. Most of us have been retired out. Returned to the real world."

Eris's brows came together in confusion. "Why not you?"

"Oh, I'm just lucky, I suppose." His laugh rang hollow. He put his elbows on his knees and regarded Eris like they were the only two people in the world. "My group was born in the real world. I've been out there. I've seen it."

Involuntarily, Eris leaned forward to the edge of her chair. "What's it like?"

"The world we see is an image of what the world used to look like. Big blue sky, all those lovely stretches of green... It's a lot of brown now. A lot of dust. The air hurts. I remember that. You had to wear a mask practically every time you went outside."

"Is there a real me, out there?" Her voice is quiet and full of fear.

"Oh, yes. All of us are real. All of this--" Cassius swung a hand broadly around "--is a little shared theater in our minds. I'm not sure what it all looks like. I like to imagine us all in stasis in the same room. It's strangely sweet."

"Gag me," Malia muttered, but she smiled.

"And when they decide they've collected enough data, they'll return us to our real lives. They'll show us the resignation of autonomy that our parents signed for us, however many decades ago. And they will use it to justify taking all the lowest people and putting them in a place like this. Because of *us*, there will be a barrier of entry just to existing."

Eris surveyed the small apartment, its

27

yellow-stained walls and scratched laminate floors. The light coming through the windows was dim but pure.

A tiny dark part of her thought this seemed better than the real world Cassius had described. But she did not know. She did not choose to be here. None of them did, not really.

"So I'm supposed to be proof that it works," Eris said. Her heart fluttered, maddened, against her ribs.

"Precisely. And then everyone they deem worthless or undesirable by God knows whose rubric will be locked up to live in their minds forever. Just carving out fake lives in places like this. Without even knowing it."

"It is kind of fucked up," Leo managed.

"But." Cassius pointed to Eris. "She can help us stop it."

"I just love your optimism," Malia said, flatly.

"I'm not proof that anything works," Eris

stammered. Her honesty surprised her. Everything in this room already felt so absurd and impossible that it didn't even feel real. It felt safe to say the things she could never say to anyone. "I'm an anxious fucking wreck. I can't even deal with normal human interactions. I spend every single day looking forward to just being asleep. If I could, I'd just be nothing. I'd sleep forever."

Cassius only grinned at her. "Precisely. You're perfect. They are tracking dopamine and cortisol, income and employment. Not your emotional day-to-day coping. That's what we need the people out there to see." He pointed to the window, as if it led to the real world.

Eris tried to hide her shock. It was a twisted kind of delight, clear and sharp as broken glass. She was exactly who they needed, exactly as she was. It was not something people told her often.

"This is all, of course, under the happy

delusion we get any administrator's attention and somehow get our story out of the test facility in the first place." Malia rose laughing without humor. "Great talk, guys. Just as productive as always."

"Don't be all moody," Graham mock-groaned.

Malia pinched at his ear as she walked by. "I'm going to hit the road. You guys keep up with the daydreaming. It's always very fun."

Leo leaned forward in the other armchair. He was not quite looking at any of them. "I might have an idea."

Eight urgent eyes turned to Leo. Malia stood gripping the door handle, staring at him.

He ventured, "They do track us. Our interactions. They want us to encounter one another." Leo gave Eris a bleak and serious look. "And once they see that you've spent the last couple of hours talking to us, they will pull you out. And they will ask you questions. As soon as they realize that you're compromised, they'll have to withdraw you from the experiment. You'll have no more test validity."

Eris rubbed anxious circles in the thigh of her jeans. She traced the strange and knotted thread of events that had brought her from happening by Cassius on the street to sitting here, listening to this insanity.

And yet she caught herself nodding along.

Malia stepped away from door. "That plan sounds like it only benefits Eris."

"We can't exactly plan a mass prison break," Cassius said through his teeth.

"It sounds like she gets to escape and the rest of us are stuck here."

Leo scowled at her. "I haven't heard you come up with anything better in the past decade or so."

She had no good retort to that but a scoff and a dismissive, "Later, kiddos," before she walked out, slamming the door behind her.

For a moment, the apartment was silent.

Then Graham looked at Eris and told her, "She's part of the group that knows their earth family and their simulated family are different."

Eris's belly dipped sickeningly. "What does that mean?"

"They wanted to test if knowing the truth of one's origins has an adverse effect." Cassius raised his beer toward the door. "And it clearly does."

"Let's kindly refrain from psychoanalyzing Malia when she's not even here to tell you all to fuck off." Graham's smile was wry as he stood and stretched. He looked down at Eris. "I have to insist on getting you something. I'm getting you water if you don't yell something at me."

"Coffee," she squeaked before Graham quite got to the kitchen. "Please."

Cassius gazed into the fire, tapping his foot restlessly. "That's what we'll do, then. Wait

32

a week and see if they come to find you." He raised his stare to Eris. The embers glowed back in his blue eyes. "If you wake up in the real world, don't forget about all of us."

Eris didn't know what he meant. She could not forget this room, these strange people, the lightness of familiarity.

Just like that, they had a plan, shoddy and simple: wait until the right moment to raise hell.

CHAPTER FIVE

The next day, Eris found Cassius waiting outside her work for her. He had his bag of crap and scowled around at all the passing A.I. that gave him strange looks. The air was so full of statistic boxes it shimmered, unnaturally.

"Are you stalking me now?" she asked. Exhaustion hung from her very bones, but she still smiled when Cassius grinned at her.

"Come on. We're going over to Graham's."

"Why?"

The old man shrugged. "Who knows how much time you have left in Oasis, little lady?" He punched her shoulder, lightly. "We want to get to know you while we've still got you around."

Eris laughed. Her family had been their normal not-quite-normal selves that morning. She felt like she sat on a knife's edge at breakfast time, doing her best to be herself. But her mother and father both gave her the same empty smiles. They did not seem to notice her fidgeting, or the worried crinkle of her eyebrows.

Part of her did not want Cassius to be right. She wanted to be crazy; that would be so much easier. But the way her parents had looked straight through her was unforgettable. Like they didn't have the right scripted reaction for her in that moment, so they simply did not react at all.

That wasn't something she would do. That wasn't something a *real* person would do.

Cassius broke her out of the spell of her thoughts. "How is your emergent existential crisis going, Eris?"

She started laughing. "What makes you ask that?"

"The look on your face." He smiled. "You're thinking pretty hard."

Eris gripped her hair with both hands and twisted it up in a tiny ponytail. Let it fall back down again. "I don't know," she admitted. "It's a lot to take in."

"You're taking it better than any other control I've met."

That made Eris's eyebrows shoot up. "You've met other controls?"

"Only a few. You're by far the most receptive." Cassius heaved his garbage bag over the other shoulder. "Most of you are set up to have an ideal, or at the very least comfortable, existence. I've even met people who've *married* A.I. in here. You can imagine no one is thrilled to hear a dirty old homeless bastard go, 'Hey, your wife isn't real!'"

That made them both laugh. They settled

down on a bus stop bench. An A.I. sat on the other end of it, and judging by the numbers on her box she was hungry or perhaps had endured a miserable day at work. Either way, she did not so much as glance up from her phone when they sat down.

"Why are you homeless?" Eris ventured.

"Well, that was a sort of shitty question to ask somebody."

Eris couldn't help her giggle. "No! I mean... the program lets you be?"

He sighed, heavily. "I burned down my house to see what would happen."

"Seriously?"

Cassius barked a laugh. "Seriously." He fished a cigarette out of his pocket and lit it. "And what happens is you're fucking homeless." He grinned at her. "So don't burn down your house, kiddo."

"Noted."

Eris sat cupping her chin in her hands and

listened to Cassius tell her stories about the outside world until the bus finally came. He kept babbling as they wove through the city, and the more he talked, the more she believed him.

He told her about his little yellow house on the corner and growing up under a sky that seemed to turn greyer and thicker every year. He told her what he could remember about his mother, how she used to smooth his hair back from his forehead every time she walked past him. How he remembered once staying up all night vomiting, and she sat holding him. They watched old black and white movies together until dawn.

It was real, and out there. Somewhere beyond the walls of her perception, a real world waited.

The idea of it made her dizzy with terror and anticipation.

***

That night, Eris stayed at Graham's apartment until nearly one in the morning. She had never been out so late. She had half-expected her parents to pester her for it, but they had stopped caring about when she came and went after she turned eighteen. As if a switch flipped in their minds and they simply stopped noticing certain things she did.

Now it made sense. They were programmed not to care, after a certain point.

The sky beyond the window was full of stars, and so too was Eris's belly full of food and a little bit of beer. She felt comfortably tipsy, just enough that every smile was thoughtless and goofy, but she could still maintain her composure. Graham was sprawled on the couch with Leo half-lying on his lap, drunk enough to keep trying to reach up and pet his beard.

"Stop it, you little fuck." Graham laughed at him, lacing his fingers through Leo's to hold his hand down. He looked up at Eris and pointed

40

his beer bottle at her with his other hand. "Hey! You don't know about the fun game we play on the bots!"

Malia grinned and licked a stray dewdrop of beer off the lip of her bottle. "What game?"

Graham gave her a meaningful look and said, "You *know.*" Then he snorted, and Leo started cackling along with him.

"Oh, my god." Malia rolled her eyes. "Graham's favorite thing is to see what weird shit you have to do or say to break the A.I."

Leo was practically shrieking with laughter. He tried to put the rest of his beer on the table and spilled the last quarter of it all over the ground. Graham picked a shirt up off the ground and threw it at the puddle, then slapped Leo's chest playfully. "Clean up your shit! You're a train wreck."

Leo rolled over groaning to mop up the floor.

Malia scoffed. "Are you both fifteen-year-old girls? Jesus, how are you already drunk?"

Cassius clutched his chest in fake shock. "Malia, aren't *you* the one who demanded we stop using girls as a pejorative?"

"I'm not! They're getting drunk with the exact same speed and tonal intensity as a pair of teenage girls." Malia gestured to the boys, then looked to Eris for support. "Right?"

"Right!" Eris's belly rose in elation. She had never felt so included. She had gotten so used to standing on the outskirts of things, faintly wondering if other people were laughing at her. It was enchanting to be part of it, to have Malia look at her as if they were two pieces of the same whole. "What do you mean you can break the bots?"

Graham started to answer, but his words dissolved into a fit of laughter.

Leo replied for him, "If you give them enough out of context actions or answers in a row, they'll just... freak out."

"It's called error mode." Cassius gave Eris a bleary smile and gestured with his beer. "And it is fairly fucking hilarious."

Eris laughed along with the rest of them until her sides hurt.

Malia drained the last of her bottle and stretched. "Well, that's it for me kids. Some of us have work tomorrow."

"On Saturday?" Cassius winced. "You do know none of this is real, right?"

"Don't even start. I don't want to be homeless and look like shit even if it is just a fake world." Malia blew him a kiss, then waved at Leo and Graham. "Make safe choices, boys. Use protection." Her stare finally settled on Eris. Her eyelids were narrow and lined with gold. "Do you want to give me company on the bus ride home?"

Eris tried not to look too eager getting to her feet.

"I can crash on your couch, right?" Cassius

said to Graham.

"You waited for the right Graham to ask. Sober-Graham says just man up and ask Blackwell to give you a new house."

That made Cassius snort. "They asked me to fill out a bullshit survey about what I learned to do differently next time. Like, what the fuck do they want from me? *Next time I'll express my anarchist vision in a way that only impacts people other than myself.*"

"I don't know." Malia jammed her feet into her work boots. "That sounds pretty damn excellent to me."

Eris waved goodbye to her new friends and followed Malia out the door. Food and beer sloshed around in her belly, filling her with nausea and delight.

Malia shoved her hands in her pockets and smiled sideways at Eris. She seemed as bright as the stars and just as lovely, even in her dirt-streaked jeans. She said, "This all must be a bit crazy for you."

She shrugged, shyly. "I think I'm starting to wrap my brain around it all." Eris tilted her head toward the sky and breathed in, deeply. "Graham told me the other day you remember the real world."

Malia's smile faded. "Parts of it."

The next words lodged themselves awkwardly in Eris's throat. She opened and closed her mouth a few times, awkwardly.

Malia laughed. "You can ask me whatever you're thinking."

A rare car drove by them, near-silent. The person inside had no statistics box, and he turned to watch them curiously as he passed. But he did not slow down. He kept driving on.

"You'd be surprised how often that happens," Malia said, catching the shock on Eris's face. "Not everyone here cares about real or not real, you know? We might as well be A.I., the way some of these people think about others."

"What do you mean?"

"I mean plenty of people here are happy the way it is. It's easy. It's comfortable." Malia stooped to pick up a rock and hurled it at a nearby street sign. It glanced off the sign with a satisfying *ding.* "But it's not living. Not really."

"How much *do* you remember?"

"About the real world?" Malia let out a long, thoughtful exhale. "Not as much as I would like to. I remember food tasted different. Better. Food in the real world is so much better." Her smile grew soft and distant. "I remember my mama. I can't remember how she sounded anymore, but I remember how her voice made me *feel.* Nothing is like hearing your own mother say your name, Eris. They can never copy that feeling."

"You must miss her."

"I miss everyone. I miss them all the fucking time." Malia put her arm around Eris's shoulders and squeezed her, briefly. "But remember: around those stupid boys, I don't have a heart."

Eris laughed. "Who's everyone?"

Malia told Eris about her big brothers, how they would torment her relentlessly when they were home, but if anyone else dared mess with her, her brothers would drop them to the fucking ground. The one time another kid tried to pick on her at elementary school, her big brothers started a falling down brawl in the middle of the school yard between themselves and the kid's friends. They had gotten themselves kicked out of school for a week, but they were bruised and grinning and proud.

"That's one of the only things I remember about them," she admitted. "I entered the Oasis when I was only seven." She shuddered. "*That* I remember, too."

"They let you remember that stuff?"

"Only my lucky little group." They finally

came to the bus stop. Malia flopped down on the bench and looked around at the silent city, disdainfully. "This all seems like a cardboard fucking play put on by kindergartners, once you know what the real world is like."

Eris sank down next to her. Tried to press for details. But as she turned her stare back around, Malia began to bleed away from her, as if she were falling backwards into nothingness. The sky opened up and swallowed everything until Eris was awash in a sea of darkness pricked with starlight.

Her belly dove for her throat. For a moment, she wondered if she was dying. If the bus had struck her out of nowhere, and this was what death felt like.

But then she remembered what Leo had said. They would pull her out of the simulation as soon as they saw the anomalies in her data. They kept careful track of their controls, after all.

Someone must have finally noticed.

CHAPTER SIX

Eris blinked, hard. When she opened her eyes again she was still sitting. Only the night and Malia and the stars had vanished. She squinted against the sudden and impossible bright.

She found herself alone in a white room. Everything was white: the table and chairs, walls and floor. Even Eris's clothes were white, a strange gown with a robe that she could not remember putting on. At once she knew this was not a dream, but not altogether reality.

Simulated. Just as fake as her bedroom and

her miserable work and the lonely litter-ridden walk to her apartment. Only this room seemed striking in its fakeness. If she closed her eyes she could imagine herself sitting in a little white box in the middle of a black ocean of nothing.

But Eris still sat in that room. The chair under her felt real as anything. The sound of the door banging open too was real enough to make her jump.

A woman walked in. Neat suit, prim blond bun. Her face was somehow clear and blurry at once. Eris could look at her, but when she blinked or looked away the woman's features melted into inscrutable vagueness.

So she tried not to blink.

The woman said in a dull and tired voice, "You must be Eris Flynn."

Eris nodded. Looked up at the ceiling, which seemed to not exist. There was just white light, stretching up into infinity.

"Am I in trouble?" Eris asked.

"No, darling. Of course not. This is just some routine work. You won't even remember it, in the morning."

"Where are we?"

The woman surveyed the little room. She was dressed in a plain blue dress and blazer. Her pantyhose torn in the knee, tiny ripple of ruined fabric. Was that a detail one would simulate?

"We're nowhere," the woman said. "A room in a building. I am your doctor."

Eris stared down at her hands, fisted tightly between her knees. She flexed her fingers and wondered if she was wrong. If this was reality itself. If the air she felt rasping in and out of her was real oxygen. If her body was even real enough to need it.

"Why am I here?" Eris asked.

"Do you have any suspicions?" She smiled, hands folded neatly in her lap. The doctor's face was unreadable.

The light overheard seemed so bright it

pulsed between Eris's temples. She swallowed, dryly. Some part of her did not want to know what was behind that door. What waited for her out in the real world.

But she thought of those numberless strangers in that lonely little apartment. Laughing at their torment because there was little else they could do.

And now she was here, facing down one of those stony-faced doctors that could only be one of their captors. The doctor's face was composed as a painting.

Eris said, "Because I know what you did to me."

The doctor offered a tight smile. "Could you clarify what you mean by that, exactly?"

"You know exactly what I mean."

"I don't like to put words in anyone's mouth. I find your perspective far more valuable."

Eris rubbed hard at her eyes. Anxiety

burned in her empty belly, but she could not stop herself from speaking. "I know you've forced me to live my life as some sort of guinea pig. I know you want to act like this little contained virtual world is the real thing, but it's not."

"Would you like to see the real world, Eris?"

Eris stared at the doctor, mouth agape. "What do you mean?"

"You could visit, if you like. Consider it a... tour."

Tears gathered in the corners of Eris's eyes. Part of her had wanted all of this to be an elaborate dream. She did not quite know what was real anymore. This room or this woman or the world she promised hulked beyond that heavy door.

Eris said, "Of course I want to go to the real world. But I can't leave all those other people trapped in there."

The doctor's smile tried on some

appearance of warmth. "This isn't about them, Eris. This is about you. I understand you have made some new friends recently. What have they told you about the world outside? That is where I'm broadcasting from, you know. I am a good person to ask about it."

Wonder dizzied Eris for a moment. She quelled the urge to reach out and touch the doctor's hand, just to feel if she was real.

She managed, "I don't know. I have heard that it's real, out there. You can feel things. Really feel them. And there are people, not just these scripts with faces. And... and..."

And you never told me about any of this. You never asked me what I thought or what I wanted.

But the doctor's smile did not crack. She only looked at Eris like she was a blubbering child, angry and senseless.

"We tried to make a world where everything is beautiful and nothing hurts. But perhaps that is difficult to appreciate, without seeing the world you were first born into."

Eris said nothing. Did not know what to say.

The doctor spoke first:

"Perhaps you would like a taste of the real world. What it's like to exist in your real body."

Anticipation churned in her belly. Eris gripped the arms of her chair. "What's the catch?"

"There is no catch. Now that you understand the intent of the hypothesis, our trial is no longer useful for its original purpose. But if you would like to try and see which existence you prefer, the option is yours." She leaned toward Eris, her smile increasingly unfriendly. "We wouldn't want you living with the question."

Eris thought of Cassius. The strange crew of friends she had met so recently and yet could not imagine leaving behind.

There would be time to bargain for them later, she decided. There would have to be. She did not have much to leverage now, anyway.

Now there was no answer she could give but, "I suppose I could see what it looks like."

CHAPTER SEVEN

Eris woke gasping and aching.

This was something she had never experienced before. She was used to *feeling*: feeling cold and heat, feeling clothing and skin brush against her body. But this was an altogether unreal sensation.

It was as if a long snake trail of roots ran down her every limb, and she could feel each little membranous branch burn and ache. As if her joints had been driven through with needles, her muscles scraped apart in the night.

This, Eris realized as she sat up, was pain.

She had felt little ghosts of it in her life, but nothing like this. Never anything like this. Her body felt as if it was trying to rend itself apart from the inside out.

The room she woke in was small, full of two dozen beds and beeping monitors. In every bed she saw the shape of some human in a deep and dreamy sleep.

Eris pushed herself up on her trembling elbows to look around. It was clinically bright, and she sat wincing in the light, struggling to collect her bearings.

A woman appeared beside her bed. The same from her dream. The same close-fitting but simple dress. The same small snag in the knee.

This was reality.

And it *hurt*.

"Welcome to the world, Eris." She extended her hand for a shake. Eris's hand slumped weak and rubbery in the doctor's grasp. She could not remember her fingers ever before feeling this dense and numb.

"It is normal to experience some muscle pain for the first few days. You have been in a coma most of your life, after all. We have used electromagnetic therapy to train your muscles to support weight while you slept, but..." She shrugged. "The pain is something we can do little about. It is the nature of muscles to tear as they heal and grow."

Eris collapsed to bury her moan in her pillow.

"I will get you something to eat," the doctor said. And then she was gone.

Eris's first meal in the real world was a bowl of oatmeal, some soggy toast, an apple, powdered orange juice. It sat thick on her tongue and tasteless. She chewed slowly, trying to compare. Trying to see if it tasted better than she was used to.

But it was just as grey and bland as oatmeal in Oasis. Or perhaps that was the way her nerves made everything taste. Anxiety did always kill her appetite.

This nurse or that flitted over to her every hour or so. Checked her vitals. Drew blood that gleamed brilliant scarlet.

After she had been awake for four hours, Eris took her first stumbling steps and instantly fell on her ass. She sat there, baffled and bewildered, as a pair of nurses helped her to her feet again.

That first day in the real world, Eris did go outside. She was pushed out by one of her nurses, a man with a kind smile who was named Titus. Eris's wrists here were so thin and pale she could see her veins almost as clearly as her bone. She had lived her life trapped in a bed, her mind eternally running in circles in some made up world, and she felt it through every inch of her body.

So Eris wilted in her chair and let herself be wheeled along. She and the nurse both wore respirators that covered their entire face, leaving two shiny portholes for the eyes. The mask was made of white leather, the suction tight and uncomfortable.

The hospital's back garden was at the end of its season. For the first time in her life Eris saw dying flowers. Rotting like an old apple left on a curb. It was strangely sad to see the roses fall into one another, their buds swollen little eyes.

She rolled one between her fingers. The petals fell off of it in a thick rainfall.

Petals and leaves and men fell here all the time. The rain fell too, in the distance; she could see the blurry dark sheets of it over the main city.

The sky overhead was a dull tawny brown, the sun a copper disc behind it. She could nearly stare right at it, with all that dust in the way.

"Why does the sky look like that?" she asked.

"It always looks like that," the nurse told

her. His voice sounded muffled and strange behind his gas mask.

The hospital sat nestled in the outskirts of a city gleaming and huge, its towering buildings disappearing into the heart of the smog. She sat with her head turned up, just watching the little lights in all the windows, wondering at the lives of the people inside.

Here, there was no box over anyone's head. The breeze carried refuse and dead leaves and stale air. People did not speak to her simply for the sake of speaking.

This cold, dark little place was reality.

She sat clutching her mask, trying to accept that.

After a few minutes, he had to take her back inside. They could not waste oxygen on standing around in the ruined air, staring at dying roses.

***

THE CONTROL GROUP

On the third day, the doctor visited her again. She wore another crisp suit. Her hair neat and perfect as before. She looked like a picture out of a magazine and not a real human.

Eris sat up in bed. Her core ached with every little movement.

The doctor said, "I don't believe I have properly introduced myself yet. I am Dr. Jane Lipton, the psychiatrist heading your case. I will introduce you soon to Dr. Smith, who is your primary physician." She presented Eris with a clipped smile. "I hope your discomfort has abated, somewhat."

Eris grimaced at her. "Yeah, thanks."

The doctor made a note on the glass tablet in her palm. The back was frosted, impossible to read. She appraised Eris like she was more a plant than a person. "Your goal, Ms. Flynn, is to decide which world you prefer: the one we have crafted for your comfort and joy, or the one that chance caused you to be born into."

Eris had a creased paperback she found on a communal bookshelf in the waiting room. An ancient book of poetry from a long-dead world. A man called Wallace Stevens. She set it in her lap to properly scowl at the doctor.

"I want my friends to be released."

"I can't talk about your friends with you, sweetie. Their information is protected." The doctor's smile was cold. "But no one is imprisoned here. No one was brought into the Oasis without their consent."

"The Oasis. That's what you call it." Eris scoffed. She could not keep the venom out of her voice. "I'm not going back. Not now. You'll have to pull me back kicking and screaming to that fucking place."

The doctor stood and cleared her throat. "Well, I assure you that will not be necessary." She folded her hands, the image of perfect calm. "Please. Stay as long as you need. We will speak again when you're ready."

THE CONTROL GROUP

Eris glared at her stiff back until the doctor was gone and Eris was alone with all the sleep-locked strangers around her.

She could not explain why she so dreaded home. It was cleaner there, sure, and perfect. And the sky so big and pure, going on forever. But she craved the imperfection and roughness of the world. The way it felt to have raw muscles and a starry mind. What realness was, more than just thought and action and existence.

It was a kind of being. Recycled oxygen in her lungs, dry petals between her fingers.

No matter how unbearable feeling became, it was better than nothing at all.

***

For the next few weeks Eris focused on rebuilding her muscles. She graduated to a walker, to crutches, and finally could shuffle about with only her cane and the slightest limp.

Her left leg could never get quite as coordinated as her right. As if it was eternally a little under stasis.

When she was alone, Eris spent countless hours in front of the mirror, seeking out differences. Trying to find some way to compare her selves. She looked nearly like herself, but there was something just off enough to make the woman in the mirror seem a stranger to her.

Every morning she rose with fire in her bones, and it was as much pain as a refusal to let it keep her rooted to that bed.

The doctor came once in a while. Watched her blankly like an owl tracking a mouse. Just to see what it would do.

But Eris was patient, and relentless. Her real body was a frail thing, but it did not have to stay that way. She rose every day and stumped down the hall of the hospital. Every step agony. She used her muscles until they shuddered so badly she had to fall gasping, the pain as real and sweet and lovely as anything she had ever known.

And with time, she was strong enough to leave.

To be her own.

***

One day, two weeks after she woke up, Eris paced the beds up and down until she found her friends. Cassius and Malia were both kept in her room, on opposite corners. Fitting that even in the real world they could barely stand to be in the same room together.

Graham and Leo she found in another corridor, where a nurse scolded her and pulled her by her aching elbow back to her own designated hall once more.

Her friends looked peaceful and perfect in sleep. Perhaps their cheeks were a little sunken, a little sallow. There was no real pain on that face. No real horror.

She cupped Malia's unmoving cheek in her hand and stared at her. Imagined her sitting up and complaining that they had wreaked hell upon her hair.

But her friends did not move.

They lay sleeping in that imaginary world, waiting for her to come along and wake them up again.

She wished there was some way to tell them she was coming as fast as she could. *Please just be patient a little longer.*

CHAPTER EIGHT

Four weeks after she first woke, she met
the psychiatrist in her office for the last time.

Dr. Lipton regarded Eris over her heavy
oak desk. "What do you feel you've learned about
the real world compared to your own?"

"It's harder." Eris stared at her palms and
laughed. "Definitely harder. I feel like I have to
earn everything so much more here, if that
makes sense."

Never once did she think she would have to
fight to learn how to walk again.

That made Dr. Lipton's smile turn

patronizing. "I know you may not be accustomed to the level of effort demanded by this universe."

"Well, due to your experiment, I have a decade or so of muscle atrophy to make up for." Eris tried to smooth her rankled hair. "That does rather complicate things."

"The limitations of a physical form," the doctor agreed. She passed a small glass tablet across the table to Eris. "Kindly fill this survey out for us, please, before we load you back into the program."

"Program?"

"Your simulation, sweetheart."

Panic shot up her throat. For a moment she could not speak around it.

Then Eris managed, "I don't want to go back."

"Why wouldn't you?"

Eris shrugged. Crammed her hands self-consciously between her knees.

The doctor set her pen down and steepled

her fingers. "Has anyone explained to you the purpose of what we do here, Eris? The whole design of this mission?"

Eris thought of Cassius, dark-eyed, spittle flying with righteous anger. She shrugged. "Sort of. I've heard stories."

"Please, let's go talk more comfortably." She stood and gestured for Eris to join her in the armchairs before the picture wall. It was a giant LCD, which Dr. Lipton currently had set to a stormy grey coast. The distant crash of waves came from the speakers drilled to the ceiling.

Eris watched the waves fall forward and backward. Told herself that this too was a kind of unrealness.

The doctor watched her for a long moment before she spoke. "Our planet is dying, Eris. I think you have seen it. A little death is normal; I know that is a strange concept, coming from your world." Another one of those damned toying smiles again.

"I know about death," Eris muttered.

"But what you don't realize is the strange ethical question facing us today. We have more people than our planet's resources can possibly hope to support. There is already too little drinking water for the world and increasingly little food. We have to find an answer that doesn't end in death." She gestured to the computer sitting at her desk. "And this is ours."

Eris's belly thrilled. She pointed at the monitor. "That's it, then? That's my world?"

Dr. Lipton peered over her reading glasses at her. "Your world is primarily digital, yes. It is an interface which we can connect to a person's neural network, allowing them to engage in this sort of... neuro-online world. It is our goal to provide people all the joy and meaning of life while preserving what is left of our planet."

Eris tried to keep the disgust off her face. "It's like living in a little paper house."

"It is better than living in a casket."

For a long moment she just stared at the doctor, open-mouthed and shocked.

That only made Dr. Lipton chuckle. "Ms. Flynn, you are hardly the first one to wake up full of rage and indignation."

"That should tell you something, don't you think?"

"Out of the ten thousand individuals that we housed here for trials, we have released nearly four thousand. And none of them have come back here asking for anything but the chance to go back again." The doctor flicked open a folder on her desk and offered the topmost sheet to Eris. "Here is the waiver of autonomy that your parents signed for you twelve years ago."

"I was *eight*."

Dr. Lipton's stare was sharp and unwavering. "There are no ethical impositions on this matter, Ms. Flynn. Your parents are allowed to surrender you for the sake of

scientific advancement. It is a noble way to live
one's life. I hope you know that."

Eris squeezed the arms of her chair tightly.
The blood pooled hot in her fingertips. *That* she
could feel. She couldn't feel her blood move in
her old body. Her muscles then were solid as
wood. It thrilled her. The pulse of something wet
and real and churning constantly within her,
hers but not hers. The only thing keeping her
alive.

There was something the false world could
never simulate: the buzz of the blood between
her ears. The way real panic felt, dizzying and
divine all at once.

Eris pushed the paper back across the desk.
"I understand you did nothing *legally* wrong. But
I want no part in it. And I know at least four
people who sorely want to retract their
involvement."

"This is old ground, Ms. Flynn. I cannot
discuss other patients' private information with

you."

"I know you can't." Eris leaned across the desk toward her. Narrowed her emerald eyes. "But I do know what you need me for. You need me to be your poster child. It would make an excellent story: simulated girl waking up to the real world and choosing the simulation once again. I know what conclusions you want to find in your research."

Dr. Lipton steepled her fingers and looked at Eris with frank concern. "What basis do you have to make such accusations?"

Eris scoffed. "Oh, plenty."

"Consider that your fears may have their real grounding in paranoia. It is traumatic on one's psyche to become accustomed to a whole new imagining of reality. Our minds are not fully built for it."

"I'm not fucking stupid, okay?" Eris jerked to her feet, clutching her cane. She slammed her fist against Dr. Lipton's desk. "I know what you're doing to me. I won't go back there."

Eris imagined it now: her wild-eyed image under a headline like **UNREAL GIRL CHOOSES UNREALITY ONCE MORE**. Dr. Lipton, smirking like it was all her triumph. Like she had trained Eris to find comfort in the perfect rows of suburbs and green lawns the way a dog felt safe in its crate.

"Please, sit. Let's finish talking."

But Eris would not. She stormed to the door as quickly as she could. Roared over her shoulder, "I'm withdrawing my consent. I want to be checked out as soon as a *real fucking medical doctor* lets me."

And then she slammed the door.

Dr. Lipton did not try to follow her.

This, she realized, was the time to raise hell.

CHAPTER NINE

A week later, Eris stood on the street with her bag of belongings. She wore an ill-fitting uniform that consisted of whatever was in the lost and found that happened to fit her.

As a gesture to her service, the program gave her an insultingly small departing recompense of five thousand dollars, a gas mask, and five filters. Eris crammed them in her pocket with a grimace.

It was early morning. The air colder than anything she had ever felt. Her breath gathered in little clouds when she breathed out and she watched it with wonder.

When Eris checked out, she received all her worldly possessions in a zippered metallic bag. Inside it she found a ragged bunny and a letter from her birth mother.

It was full of ragged apologies and fifty dollars. Eris read it over and over again, trying to know it as well as her new heartbeat. Then she folded it up and tucked it carefully in her sweater pocket.

The world, huge and grey as it was, was hers to make of it what she could.

When she was leaving the hospital, the nurse Titus had stopped her. He'd pushed a flier into her hand. "A bunch of ex-Oasis members like to get together every couple of weeks and just... vent, you know? It's good for the soul. They're meeting tonight, if you wanted to try to go."

Eris had taken it with a weary smile. Then, before she left, she turned and gave the nurse a brief, tight hug. Murmured, "Thank you," into his shoulder. She did not have any daggers for Titus. He had walked her to and from the bathroom without a single rude word too many times for her to hate him.

Now the wind bit through her cheap stained coat. Eris stared down at the flier and resolved to find out where, exactly, the Franklin Civic Center was.

***

Eris arrived to find that the support group for Oasis survivors met in a small room in the back of the civic center. They had stale coffee and these little round cookies that Eris could probably eat thirty of.

The room was full of strangers of all ages. They all seemed more or less normal. For a moment she just stood there in the doorway, crippled by the shock of sharing a room with so many real *humans.*

Certainly, she had spent a month surrounded by them. But two dozen people in induced comas hardly made substantial conversation partners.

A man rose to greet her. Shook her hand, warmly. "Welcome!" he said. "You can call me Novak."

Eris mumbled her name.

"You look like you're fresh out." His tone was light and reassuring as a blanket. He was dark-eyed and dark-haired, but his face so bright he made her smile despite herself.

"Quite literally," Eris admitted. She surveyed the group of people. "Is everyone here from out of Oasis?"

"Sure. There's a strong community around the Blackwell area, as you can imagine." He nodded over his shoulder and Eris followed. He showed her to an empty chair and sat down beside her.

THE CONTROL GROUP

Eris could have talked to him forever. He had the kind of smile that was constant and relentless. But as soon as she sat he leaned forward, elbows on his knees, and announced, "We have a new member joining us at group this evening."

She crumpled into herself, burying her face in her palms. Barely suppressed the urge to groan, *Oh, I hate this kind of shit.*

"Eris! Would you like to tell us a little about yourself?"

She resisted the urge to puddle into her chair. Instead Eris sat on her shuddering hands and felt the ring of strangers stare at her.

They could not be that frightening. After all, they had done the same thing she had: stumbled out of bed, clumsy and helpless as babies. Relearned how to live in this strange new world.

Eris did not let her stare fall to the floor. She met the eyes of all these strangers one by one and said, "I was just let out of the hospital today."

"What's your rebirthday?" a woman across the room interrupted.

Eris gaped at her until the group leader Novak clarified, "The day you woke up in the real world," then said to the woman, "Agnes, please. I love your input, but..."

"You're right! You're right. My bad habit."

"Uh." Eris looked around uncertainly. "I've been here six weeks. I haven't seen much. To be honest, I've only been out a few hours." She swallowed the thick lump of anxiety constricting her throat. "But I have seen enough to know that we should be doing something. There are still people trapped inside there, you know."

"Oh, this again." An older man a few seats to her left slapped his hat scornfully against his knee. "Like it's all sunshine and roses out here. At least they don't know what it feels to be hungry."

"They don't know what it feels to be *anything*," Eris shot back.

"Hey, let's be civil."

"I am being civil. I'm only out here to get my friends out. And if all of you guys really came out of Oasis, I don't understand how you can just sit down here talking about yourselves while so many people are still trapped in there."

Eris's words fell heavily, like a tower of collapsing bricks. For a long minute no one said anything at all.

Then Novak patted her shoulder. "All of us understand your frustration. Honestly. Many of the people here left friends and family behind in the Oasis. But there's nothing we can do."

"Have you even tried?"

Novak's look became thoughtful. He glanced around the circle of faces, some of them tense, some worried, others teetering on enraged. He murmured to Eris, "Perhaps we should discuss this after the meeting."

Eris could concede to that. She sat with her arms folded over her chest, listening to the stories of so many strangers. The old man who had snapped at her was twenty months into his job search. No one would hire someone who had been in stasis for as long as he had. Sixty years of dreamy darkness was simply unheard of. Too many health issues, too much cultural disconnect.

Who would take that on? All risk and no reward.

Eris suddenly understood why he had glowered at her suggestion that the Oasis was a trap. For some it really was just that: an oasis. An escape from the callousness of the real world.

She sat silent, wrestling with that, while the others spoke.

Perhaps the neighbors were all characters with cardboard smiles, but they did smile, and they invited you over to dinners you could really attend, if you bothered.

That she didn't see in the smoke-blackened sky or the tight faces of these strangers.

Eris waited until the others filtered out to speak to Novak. The room seemed so much larger with only two people in it.

This time, when he looked at her, she sought his eyes. They were a calm and deep brown. His smile curled when he caught her staring. "What are you thinking about, Eris?"

"My friends," she lied. Eyes did not look that way, in the Oasis. They did not look so boundless and full of light.

"It's a sensitive topic around here. I know you haven't been here long enough to really acquaint yourself with the politics." He winked. Began shoving folders and clipboards in his worn messenger bag. "But you're not the first one to roll out of bed and start demanding that Blackwell let everyone go."

"Then why haven't they?"

"They don't have to. The people in there haven't demanded it. So they don't have to do anything."

"They *have*. No one is listening."

Novak paused. His brows crinkled in uncertainty. "There may be a way to help your friends."

"Really?" Eris bolted to her feet and swayed unsteadily. She realized that she had not eaten anything but cookies and water for seven hours now. It was not like in the Oasis, when she had a little chirping alarm at the back of her mind reminding her when her belly was empty. Now she had only herself to trust.

Novak caught her arm. "Jesus. Are you okay?"

"I'm fine. Just a little... new to things." She gestured to her whole self. Hoped he would understand.

"Do you have somewhere to stay tonight?"

Eris paused, sizing him up. Then she shook her head and admitted, "Didn't plan that far ahead yet."

Novak shouldered his bag and shrugged. "I could offer you a couch, if you want. It's reasonably comfortable."

She wanted to argue with him. Wanted to insist that she would do nothing until all four of her strange new friends were walking in this world with her.

But she was so tired her very bones ached. Her stomach so empty that her brain was nothing but the constant vague desire for food.

Eris admitted, "I would love that."

***

She helped Novak cook dinner. They made a stir fry with pseduo-chicken, Novak's fond name for lab-grown chicken breast, with leftover rice and carrots and peas and little pieces of garlic that Eris cut too big.

Novak showed her how to use a knife. She understood the mechanics of it from her world, but the physics were all off. She was not used to the resistance of real food. Her garlic kept skittering across the cutting board.

They ate and talked.

"I grew up in the Oasis, you know. My parents signed me over to Blackwell when I was six."

"*Why?*"

Novak laughed. "So I wouldn't starve to death? You know our parents didn't sign us away to a place like that as a *first* resort."

Eris chewed her food numbly and thought and thought. She finally said, "So what do you think of the whole thing? Oasis?"

He thought over that question a moment as he chased his rice with his fork. Then he said, "I know a lot of people wanted out, but there was a time when everyone wanted in. More people

88

than they could even let in."

"Why?"

"Famine." He let that word hang on the air. Did not elaborate beyond, "Neither of my parents survived it." Then Novak clapped his hands together and offered her another cheery smile. "In the morning, we will see about trying to get your friends out. I know of a process to apply for an individual's autonomy to be manually re-evaluated. It requires Blackwell to pull a patient out of the simulation and check in with them."

Relief lapped like cool water over her heart. It would not save everyone, but it could save her friends. And that would have to be a good enough start.

Cassius was the persuasive one, anyway. The one with all the fire and rage. He could do the hard work, when he got out. Rally the masses. Upend the statues, or whatever.

Eris nodded again and again. A part of her

wanted to cry out of gratitude and joy, all the stress of the past few weeks releasing like steam.

But she swallowed her tears and ate her stir fry and went to bed on Novak's couch. His blanket smelled faintly musky, exactly like him. She lay there for a long time, just inhaling his scent.

Another thing the Oasis did not have: the sweet earth scent of another human. She never knew until she laid there in the dark that smells could hold secrets and longing.

Her dreams were full of people she barely knew and yet loved with all her heart.

CHAPTER TEN

True to his word, Novak brought Eris to Blackwell Industry's main offices downtown. He had no car, but he led the way with practiced ease to the train station.

Her little pretend city had been so orderly and clean compared to this place. Grime seemed to adhere to the city like a second skin. The air sagged against the buildings and coated them in sticky fingers of soot.

Eris did her best not to touch anything. "All the trains travel underground now," he explained as he plunked down the steps ahead of her, his heavy bag rattling against his back. "Makes for less traffic congestion, street-side."

"Right," Eris said, like she understood. In Oasis all the cars simply... went. There was no honking or cursing or running stoplights.

This purely human version of the city was a different beast altogether. The roaring sound of it was so cacophonous that Eris would have simply curled up there with her hands clasped over her ears if Novak was not walking beside her, looking back to see if she was following.

Even under his gas mask, his smile was honeyed. Lingering.

The train that came for them was a fine and perfectly smooth cone. Its sleek modern nose speckled with flies and filth.

It whisked them away, under the city.

The train car seemed nearly as streaked with dirt and graffiti as it had been outside. The cab was crammed to bursting with humans. Eris tried not to openly stare. Class certainly existed in her world, and some of these people looked wealthy. But most of them looked as haggard and poor as Cassius had been the day she turned her head and caught him looking at her.

For a moment, she could see nothing but her friends' slack sleeping faces. Eris dug the heels of her hands into her temples until the memory went away again.

Twenty minutes later, they arrived outside a squat grey building with heavy steel doors. Its lower windows were barred, its door so heavy that Eris had to heave her whole body back against it to open it.

A sign at the door advised visitors that the building featured filtered air. Eris tugged off her mask with a gasp of relief.

Almost every surface inside was glossy, sharp-cornered, and perfectly smooth. The lobby felt like the inside of a finely designed fishbowl. Eris stood head turned up, staring around, as Novak went to speak to the front desk.

Even the ceiling was intricate. An etching of prisms, their sides done in varying angles in the gold plating. The light caught them in different ways every time Eris twisted her head.

Novak tapped her elbow. "Come on," he told her. "We're a little late for our appointment."

***

They sat in a small office, nearly as grand as the lobby. The man behind it was finely coiffed too, his black hair combed to an immaculate edge. He pulled a file off of the perfect stack on his desk and flipped it open.

He presented his hand and a crisp white smile. "You must be Eris."

Eris shook his hand, slowly. Everything here looked too much like Oasis. That was what made her stare linger. The strange familiarity of it. It was a distinct style, all hard edges and bright colors. They made their building look like the imaginary world she had always called home.

She and Novak seated themselves in the two uncomfortable little leather chairs before the man's desk.

He introduced himself as Peter Malone. Clicked his pen a few times as he looked over the single page in Eris's file. "How can I help you today, Ms. Flynn?" He looked to Novak. "And this is your...?"

"Friend," he supplied.

Novak's sideways smile brought a rush of blood to Eris's cheeks. She nodded in agreement. "I came here because I know four people who need to their autonomy reassessed. I met them, in the Oasis. They want to get out."

"There is a means within the system that they can request that." His smile was half a grimace now. "It is not really our protocol to initiate these procedures from the outside world. It threatens the test's internal validity."

"Well, you *do* have a process for initiating it." Novak looked dark, unimpressed. As if he had anticipated this wavering. "And we have come here to initiate that process."

Now Peter was not smiling. He turned to his computer and said, "Of course. Do note that it can take four to six months to process such requests, and we do need a sufficient amount of information to make the application."

Novak sank back into the chair, arms folded over his chest. As serene and immovable as a boulder. "That's fine. We have all the time in the world."

Four to six months made panic tornado behind Eris's eyes, but she said nothing. When they got out, when she told them the story, they would understand. They would laugh with her. They would say thank you.

She looked between Novak and Peter. Watching their lips move but barely listening anymore. There was only this constant dreadful whisper at the back of her mind: *you're doing all this for people who don't even like you, really. Don't even know you.*

But they were the only friends she had. And they were waiting for her.

Novak nudged her shoulder, lightly. Eris snapped her eyes to him, and he smiled at her. "Hey," he murmured. "Are you okay?"

She looked around. The Blackwell representative was gone, the office door hanging open.

"He went to go make some copies. Turns out they do this one on paper, still." He tilted his head, trying to catch her eye. "Are you alright, Eris? You seem a bit... in your head."

"It's a long time to wait."

"There's little else to do."

Eris wasn't sure she believed that. She sat biting her nail and thinking, hard.

***

Eris and Novak spent nearly the entire day at the Blackwell office. She told her story a few different times to a few different people. Each time sighing a little more than the last.

Novak told her on the train ride home that they were trying to check for consistency. The engines bellowed and a group of drunk girls near them cackled, so Novak had to press his mouth against her ear for her to hear. The clouds of his breath made her skin prickle in delight.

He said, "They claim it's to help avoid false reports, but I think it's to find arbitrary reasons for denial, to be honest."

Eris nodded along. She wished she knew how to keep a conversation going, to keep him close there. She had never felt anyone so real and so close.

Then, she turned her chin towards his ear and murmured to him, "How did you get out?"

Novak's eyebrows quirked in lovely confusion. "Sorry?"

"Out of the Oasis."

"Oh, I was scheduled out a couple of years ago. They are planning to shut the program down within the next five years and release their final report on it." Novak sighed through his teeth. "You haven't heard my anti-Blackwell rant yet. Don't worry, you won't have to be around me too much longer to hear plenty."

"I think I'd like your rants." Eris could not help her rising smile. "My grumpiest friend from there told me that they're using it for, like, casual evil or something."

"Casual evil is an excellent descriptor. It's always dangerous when a company starts an experiment with a certain outcome in mind." His look soured. "They would do anything they can to maintain expectations."

They spent the rest of the train ride in silence.

That night, after they finished cooking and eating and talking and cleaning, Eris and Novak sat together in the living room, watching his television.

And she asked him, "Do you have a video camera?"

"Kind of a shitty one, but yeah. Why?"

Eris only smiled and told him, "I think I need it."

And after Novak went to bed, Eris turned on the lights and the camera and sat before it.

She told her friends' story again. Her story.

Only this time, she told it for everyone to hear.

CHAPTER ELEVEN

The woman in the video was not what anyone expected when they thought of an Oasis patient.

She was not sickly or strange or confused, the sort of odd person you would prefer not to encounter alone at night. She was thin and lovely as a flower in autumn. Her voice was as clear and sharp as her green eyes, which barely wavered from the camera.

You could see the rage coiled behind her tongue. Bundled up in her every word.

She began, "I'm not supposed to tell you

any of this. But my name is Eris Flynn. I am part of the control group. My mother volunteered me when I was eight years old. I lived in the Oasis for twelve years and had no idea what it was. I'm the kind of person that Blackwell Industries wants to turn at least four billion of you into."

Her scowl deepened and darkened. "I'll tell you what the Oasis is really like."

***

Last night when Novak had handed her the camera, he had worn this deliciously mixed look on his face. Eris had not yet gotten accustomed to how *complicated* humans could look. The A.I. had a limited emotional range, comparatively. They could do angry or sad but not angry and sad.

This look was worry and excitement at once. Like Novak too couldn't decide how he felt about what he was about to say. "I don't know what you want this for," he had said, "but you should know that we're not supposed to talk about what we through in there."

Eris had frowned up at him. "Why shouldn't I?"

"Oh, I never said you shouldn't. But Blackwell will come after you. Legally. And otherwise, if that doesn't work. I subscribe to the particular conspiracy theory that they killed the last person who tried what you're doing." And he set the camera in her hands. "So do what you need to do. Honestly, I hope you do exactly what I think you're planning. But you should know what you're getting into."

The camera had felt heavy suddenly. Like she was cradling her whole future in her arms.

Now it was morning. Her video had been out in the world for seventeen hours and already over two hundred million people had watched it.

Eris sat in Novak's living room, watching her video play out on the news screen over and over again. It had become viral in a way she had never anticipated.

No one from the control group had spoken out before. Blackwell had their own testimonies from smiling people recorded in a digital world, who claimed that knowing the truth had made them love their fake world even more.

A news anchor in a sheeny grey blazer occupied half the screen beside Eris's video. She paused the video and said, "Now here she references Caleb Jackson, whose unfortunate death was ultimately ruled an accident. He was, as many recall, run over the day he was meant to testify against Blackwell when an automated city bus malfunctioned and struck him."

"A Sunny Cities bus, which is owned by Blackwell." Novak appeared suddenly over the back of the couch, sipping coffee. He offered a mug to Eris--milk and sugar, just as she liked it. She accepted it gratefully. "They like to keep that detail out."

THE CONTROL GROUP

Eris held up a hand and shushed him, her eyes never leaving the screen. He squeezed her fingers, which delighted and surprised her. She squeezed them back without even realizing it.

"I'm awfully proud of you, you know," he said. "I couldn't do what you did. Hell, I haven't."

She didn't look away from the television. "I'm not doing it for me. And that helps."

Novak settled onto the couch next to her. She had the strange compulsion to reach out and touch him again. To fill the spaces between her fingers with his. She did not know if she liked him, exactly. But she wanted to be around him. She wanted to know his mind as well as her own.

Another feeling the Oasis lacked: *attraction.* The kind you could feel in your very fingers.

But the reporter stopped talking, and they began replaying her tape again. They were at the end, when she reached the cusp of her rant:

"You are signing up to let a group of strangers decide who lives and who waits in a room to die. There is no Oasis. There is only anxiety and alienation and the constant sense that nothing is quite right with your world or your family or your own body. There is no place you can pile up all the people you don't like. We have to exist, together, somehow."

Her voice tightened. Broke. "And goddammit, you have to let them all *out.* There are people trapped there, right now, by a corporation hiding behind paperwork and bull[censored]. And you're all just letting it happen."

The video stopped on Eris's face, twisted in disgust. Frozen there, for millions to see.

"It's quite an inflammatory statement." The reporter spread her hands and said, "What do you think? Is her case legitimate? We bring in Dr. Jane Lipton, who was the psychiatrist at the head of Eris Flynn's case."

The television cut to Dr. Lipton: perfect blond bun and fine crimson suit. Fear turned like nausea in Eris's belly.

"What is your professional opinion, Dr. Lipton? This woman claims to be effectively traumatized by your program. You worked with her personally."

"Yes, for the better part of the past month I saw her nearly every day."

"Barely," Eris muttered under her breath. She clutched her coffee mug so tightly her knuckles whitened.

"Maybe we should turn this off," Novak started, but Eris waved him away.

"I need to know what they think." She turned her sharpened glare on Novak. "If they're really so dangerous."

The reporter was saying, "Has any other member of the control group been released to the general public?"

"Several dozen, yes. Primarily individuals

like Ms. Flynn, whose individual trials were corrupted. Theirs is the longest-running of our experiments, for obvious reasons, as it takes some years to chart efficacy over an entire lifetime." Her smile was thin and foreign to her.

"But none other have spoken out before," the reporter clarified.

"No. Not yet."

"So her testimony is... certainly not a hopeful predictor for your program's aim to provide a humane life alternative."

Dr. Lipton removed her glasses and leaned toward the camera with a tired sigh. "I do not believe Eris Flynn to be a credible witness. She presented as a highly paranoid young woman. She was convinced we are attempting to imprison her fellow patients within the Oasis. It is well established that there is a reporting system within the program that allows the patient to withdraw themselves at any time, as well as a mechanism to trigger this from the outside world. In fact, she initiated four such requests for her friends. And yet she releases the video the same day we begin our investigation, with no acknowledgment of Blackwell's full cooperation in her cause."

Eris nearly threw whatever she was holding at the television out of sheer rage until she remembered it was coffee.

Novak reached for the remote.

"Don't turn that shit off."

"Eris. This is all making you crazy."

She stared at him. Felt something in her distending like a rubber band about to snap.

"I'm not crazy," she said.

"You know that's not what I meant."

"I don't know that." She set her mug down on the table and began to pace around the couch. Eyes glued to Dr. Lipton's insufferable smirk. "She doesn't get it. It has nothing to do with her stupid request forms. The whole system is fucked. The whole *thing*. And we're just one little piece of it. It hardly even matters if I get my friends out if that bitch still gets to come on TV and tell everyone how great the Oasis is."

Her head buzzed with anger and low oxygen. Eris did not even realize Novak had muted the television until she stopped talking long enough to breathe.

"Why did you mute that?" she demanded.

"Uh, because of what you're doing right now?" Novak watched her, brow creased in worry. "Don't let her wind you up. She knows you're watching. She wants you to react."

"But she's just sitting there saying all this obvious garbage about me—"

"Exactly. It's obvious, and garbage. So don't make a weird ranting video confirming everything she's accusing you of. Okay?"

That calmed the storm in Eris's belly. She nodded, slowly.

"Okay," she managed.

"The only things we're going to do are

watch and wait." Novak stood and held out his arms to her. His smile was small, full of pity and understanding. Eris paused before sinking into the hug. She collapsed into him there for a moment, just marveling at the feeling of being enveloped in another's whole person.

"Wow," she said, despite herself. Embarrassed heat instantly flooded her cheeks when she realized she'd said it aloud.

"No, Oasis-hugs are unbelievably shitty," he said in her ear. "I agree."

And then he pulled away, and Eris was alone with the ghost of a feeling.

Novak nodded toward the kitchen. "Help me make breakfast." Eris gestured to her coffee mug, and he laughed. "That's not breakfast."

Eris tried, but she could not forget herself in the cool morning light or Novak's constant probing smile. She could think of nothing but a world that was real and not real at once. Her friends, knotted up inside of it. Waiting for her.

THE CONTROL GROUP

She hoped they could wait a little longer.

CHAPTER TWELVE

Silence was difficult and choking, but Eris
did it. For two long weeks, she sat in Novak's
apartment and did nearly nothing but watch the
news and hold her tongue.

The day after she posted the video, a grim-
faced man in a raincoat knocked on Novak's
door. Eris had been alone, and she had opened
the door and stared at him, panic blooming in
the back of her mind.

"Are you Eris Flynn?" he asked.

"Yes," she said.

He handed her a parcel full of papers and

left. A thick stack of legal documents from Blackwell: her original contract, the non-disclosure agreement highlighted for her attention. A cease and desist letter on thick paper, a neat letterhead.

Eris threw it in the recycling. Novak pulled it out and lectured her about it later. How a paper trail was vital even if she disagreed with what it said.

Novak made her go out with him, when he went out. Oasis recovery group sessions, the grocery store, early morning walks around the city. No one went for walks but Novak. It seemed when she and Novak passed other people on the street, their masked faces were always down-turned. Always hurrying from one place to the next like mice fleeing rain.

But Novak walked looking at the yellow sinking sky. She could not see his mouth behind his mask, but she could see by the crinkle of his eyes that he was smiling. At the filthy buildings, the ruined air. At her.

The television roared about her for a few days, and then seemed to forget. But the internet did not. She did not know how many hours she spent curled up on Novak's laptop in his living room, scanning through forums and discussion threads. Reading what people thought of her. Every once in a while, she would see one or two people claiming to be from Oasis themselves. Validating or invalidating her.

Only once, she saw another control. She made an account and sent them a message, but they never responded.

Nearly everyone in the world knew her face after that video, but Eris felt alone in a way she never had before. The leaves kept browning and falling, and the air got colder every day, but she heard nothing else from Blackwell. Nothing about her friends.

Four to six months rattled around her mind like a loose marble. If she waited four months, would anyone care? Would anyone listen to her a second time?

It was fifteen days since she recorded her video. A cool Friday morning, the sky so wet and clear it nearly looked blue. Eris sat staring at her account for the video: iamerisflynn. She had a few million followers already. All over one video, which the website had removed anyway. She couldn't guess how many of those were spectators and how many were on her side.

But still.

She set up the camera.

If she could not tap into the public's underlying discontent, she would have to manufacture some.

***

When Novak came home, he was sheet white and staring at Eris in mute horror. He held up his phone. Her second video already playing.

"Did you really do this? Are you serious?"

"Very." She tapped away at his keyboard.

Didn't even pause to look at him. "I'm not playing any more waiting games, Novak."

From Novak's tinny little phone speakers, she could hear herself saying, "*Tomorrow morning we will march and rally around Blackwell's main offices in Seattle—*"

Then he shut his phone off and scowled at her. First real look of frustration she had ever seen from him. "I really wish you had talked to me first, Eris."

She blinked. Color flooded her cheeks. "Why?"

"You don't have much room to fuck up, that's why. You're representing everyone now."

"It's only like forty seconds."

"Yes, forty antagonizing seconds of you planning an illegal demonstration. That a *lot* of people have seen," Novak pressed his head in his hands and sighed. Dropped his swollen messenger bag on the floor beside the couch and flopped down next to her. "I know you're trying to make yourself unignorable, but you're just going to piss someone off."

"Good. More people should be pissed off."

"Yes, but you're pissing off the *wrong* people, Eris." He regarded her tiredly. "I just worry for you. I want you to be safe."

"Of course I'm safe."

"Blackwell is a federally funded institution. You're not just taking on your doctor or a private corporation. You're taking on the American Empire and a federally incorporated company, here. Publicly and aggressively. You're like throwing rocks at a bear."

Eris frowned at him. "Did you have a bad day or something?"

"This has nothing to do with me." Novak sighed again. Rubbed hard at his face. Another new combination: anger and worry and fear. "You're my friend. I don't like to see you purposefully drawing targets on your back."

"But you'll go with me, tomorrow."

"What is your plan, exactly?"

She smirked. "Hell-raising."

"Well, that's not exactly a plan," Novak said, but he was smiling now, begrudgingly.

They sat up talking and strategizing well into the night.

***

In the morning Eris woke to find she and Novak had fallen asleep on the couch in a swamp of notes and plans and mostly-finished posters. They had made a huge stack of them for people to collect and carry as they showed up. Novak was using the curled up sheets of unused poster board like a pillow.

Part of her wanted to just sit there watching him for a moment. The soft line of his brow. His half-open mouth. All sleeping people in Oasis looked the same to her. All of her family laid still as stones after their heads hit the pillow.

119

Only she tossed and turned and made faces in the night. But Novak made her feel normal and human.

She leaned over and shook his shoulder.

"Hey," she whispered. Delighted at the sleepy start in his eyes when he turned to look at her.

"Oh, shit," he said without moving. "I can already feel that my back *hates* me for this."

"Get up, old man." That made Novak open one sleepy eye to glare at her. Unspoken counterargument: *I'm barely older than you.* "We have to be there in two hours and you have a lot more posters to make for me."

They spent every second before the rally scrambling to gather paper and posters and stakes and signs. Novak brewed a ten-gallon jug of hot tea which he carried along with a bag full of paper cups.

They arrived outside Blackwell half an hour early. And already dozens of people crowded out front, absently milling about. The security guards stood by awkward, hands on hips. Trying to decide if the bystanders should be shooed away from the sidewalk.

Eris hesitated there on the corner, her arms full of signs, belly full of fear and hope.

Novak nudged her in the back with the jug, lightly. "Come on," he said. "There's certainly no going back now."

They walked together down into the rally.

CHAPTER THIRTEEN

Blackwell Industries headquarters stretched so high Eris could not see its very top beyond the fog today. It was a damp and icy morning, but by the time she finished handing out tea and introducing herself to the first fifty or sixty people there, another dozen or two had come.

Eris was running out of little cups and tea, but it did not matter. Most people just wanted to see her. She had never seen someone marvel at her, but it seemed like half these people came just to see if she was real. If her story was true.

Some people even pushed their masks up halfway, and she copied them, just to hear and see each other beyond the masks' thick ventilation.

Novak stood with the empty tea jug at the fifty-foot boundary line they could not cross, where the headquarters' private property began, politely prompting people back to the appropriate half of the sidewalk. He kept glancing worriedly at the police cars parked across the street, just waiting for them to become disorderly. But whenever he noticed Eris look over at him, he offered her a reassuring smile.

The more people gathered, the more Eris realized she had underestimated this. She grabbed a few of the people who had been there since she arrived and gave them a list of things to get. To her surprise they returned within fifteen or twenty minutes with everything she needed.

A kitchen step stool. A megaphone. A

change of clothes, if she needed to get away fast.

Eris had imagined one or two hundred people. Small enough to shout at. She had hoped to escalate, to plan for a large event more slowly.

By the time the demonstration was meant to start, the whole block was full of people and so loud Eris could not even think straight. Everyone's voices stacked one on top the next. There seemed to be a thousand people at least. They spilled over onto the neighboring blocks, into the street. Officers with shields and vests tried to usher people out of the road, but there were too many people and nowhere else to go.

And Eris stood in the center of it, before Blackwell's doors. She set up the step stool and climbed atop it. Surveyed the swarm of gas masks assembled before her. Some were painted, which filled Eris with a feathery hope. There were still lovely things. The world was still lovely, even now.

The stool did not grant her much height.

She stood only three or four feet above the others. But it gathered the crowd's attention, easily. The police's, too. She stood in the gaze of thousands of eyes, dozens of cameras, and pulled off her mask.

Lungs full of reeking air, she said, "Blackwell is not here to save us all. It is here to imprison us arbitrarily, and make existence itself something you must *earn*. There may be many of us, but our lives are still worth enough not to hand that kind of power over to just anyone."

For a moment, in the back of her mind, Eris was in the living room with Novak. Drafting opening lines. And he was laughing at her, saying, *No, you can't call Blackwell a "dirty fucking corporation".*

"I'm sure many of you have bought into the marketing. It is effective. They'll save the world without all the pain of death. But living in there is like being a rat in a box forever." Eris turned to see more police cars gathering. Novak gesturing for her to stop. "One out of every two of you will get to know what that's like, if you leave here today and do *nothing.* That is Blackwell's plan for your world. That is what your community's passivity and disinterest is allowing."

She knew she should step down. Those were riot police.

But she could not end there.

Eris blurted out, "So make them *care.* Make them uncomfortable. Make them *notice.* Don't let this indecency stand just because it seems nearly normal. If we oppose it, they cannot enact it. But if you do nothing, you're signing yourselves up for a life in a virtual coffin." The police were lining up, their shields like scales of a thick plastic hide. "It seems I have to run. Be loud! Be fucking angry! End the Oasis program!"

And then Eris bolted off the step stool. She handed her megaphone off to the girl who first had given it to her. The crowd was frenzied, and Eris saw why. The police had begun to move in, shields raised.

Novak gripped her elbow.

"Where's your tea thing?" she asked him.

"You're seriously worried about that right now? We need to *run*."

Eris ran, her borrowed backpack clattering against her back. The crowd was confused now, and clogged. Starting to press toward the building. One of the Blackwell security guards tried to grab Eris's arm, but she kicked at him and he shied back in shock.

Then she and Novak burrowed through the crowd. She just gripped his arm, let him lead the way out. She had not taken the time to put her mask back on. It still rattled around her neck. The thick air made her throat swollen and raw.

But she followed Novak. To her surprise, he did not take her to the subway station.

"They'll be checking the exits," he told

her, low, under his breath, "because you had to do the *really* inflammatory one we agreed you wouldn't do."

"The best one," she corrected.

"Yes, the criminal one, Eris. The one inciting public discord."

They reached a break in the crowd, and Eris paused to fasten her gas mask back on. She was suddenly grateful for the strange plastic aftertaste the filters gave the air. It was better than what they took out.

Someone tapped her shoulder.

Novak said, sharp, "Sorry, we don't have time," but Eris waved him off. Distantly, she heard the pop of rubber bullets and people shrieking.

"You're the megaphone girl," Eris said, her face splitting in a smile. She couldn't remember the girl's name, but Eris knew she had been out of the Oasis for two years herself.

"I am," she said. "Come on. I got you a

getaway car, too."

Eris passed Novak a hopeful smile. He looked at her, red-cheeked, trying to hide his fear.

"We don't have much else," he muttered.

She and Novak followed the girl into the panicking crowd.

CHAPTER FOURTEEN

Eris and Novak chased the girl through the knots of protest traffic. The crowd had a new volume, a new kind of urgency. Screams filled the air as people pushed and ran past each other, trying to put as much distance between themselves and the wall of marching shields as possible.

But this girl shoved against the current. Heading back toward the police.

Eris called after her, "You're going the wrong way."

"No," the girl said, not even stopping. Not

even quite looking over her shoulder. "You follow me or you get arrested."

So Eris shut her mouth and followed her.

As she ran strangers' voices drained in and out of her, rising and falling: *is that—are you— you're that girl—that's the control—from the speech.* Eris ignored them, shrugged off the people who tried to stop her.

She was close enough to see the riot police over the shoulders of the people trying to flee past her. Heavy vests and thick shields, gas masks black and thick as their helmets. The sun gleamed off the perfect round circles of their eyes. They looked like ants, and Eris realized her mask must look the same to them.

Except the police carried guns, and she had only a backpack and a belly full of fear.

Novak prodded her back, and she kept going.

The girl with the megaphone pushed perpendicularly across the current of people until she reached a sliver of an alleyway between two buildings.

Novak froze there at the alley's opening. "I don't know, Eris," he started.

But she only scoffed at him, "What are you doing? *Run*," so he sighed and followed her.

At the end of the alley there was a car. So old it still had a pair of metal license plates instead of an electronic signature. The blue paint had gone piebald with rust. The driver's side sagged worryingly low.

Eris and Novak dove into the backseat after the girl. Eris found herself in the wedge of the middle seat, leg pressed to Novak's, falling into his side as the girl leaned forward and slapped the driver's shoulder, shouting in his ear, "*Go!*"

Then the car jerked and jolted and sped out of the alley. They came out on a street that Eris didn't recognize and began heading north, away from the city center. It was only a handful of blocks away from the police and the terrified crowd, but for a few crystal seconds this street seemed perfectly calm.

For a moment, Eris thought she really was safe that easily.

A trail of police SUVs with shiny metal hides came roaring around the corner, lights flashing soundlessly. Eris hunkered down low in the car, huddled over Novak's lap, but no one noticed her in that rusting shuddering little car. The police just raced each other to Blackwell Industries.

"They're going to try to build a barrier to stop you from getting out," the girl said.

Eris sat up, glancing around anxiously. She tried to focus enough to find the right thing to say. Her mind felt like a drawer tossed upside down, all its contents scattered across the floor of the car. Finally she just managed, "What do you mean?"

"That's what my uncle said they'd do." She nodded to the driver, who didn't turn his head at his mention. "That's what they do, when they think you're still in the area. They're going to shut down the bridges. Lock down the city. My uncle said we'd just hole up until they gave up looking."

The driver glanced at them all in the rear view mirror and offered a ghost of a smile.

"Thank you," Novak said, "to both of you." He sounded distant and cold and full of fear.

"It's nothing," the girl answered for both of them. She tugged on the handle of the backpack still stuck tightly to Eris's back. "You need to change. Fast."

Eris wrestled the clothes out of the bag. Swapped sweaters, slipped off her jeans and put on the grey leggings inside. There was a hat, a pair of glasses that were definitely prescription. Wearing them made Eris's head spin. But she put them on and stuffed all her pale hair under her hat. She tried to look at herself in the rear view mirror. She thought she looked like herself but in a hat and glasses, but she hoped she would be unrecognizable.

"I can't remember your name," Eris admitted to the girl.

She grinned at Eris, then threw Eris's clothes out the window. "Diane," she said. "And that's my uncle, Virgil." She leaned forward again, tapped the man's shoulder. He glanced at her out of the corner of his eye. She signed as she spoke, "Say hi." Her fingers danced briefly in front of her mouth for **say**, then a small wave for **hi**.

He raised his hand back and waved at them all.

"Good to meet you both." Novak's eyes burned with questions but he said nothing else. Just held his tight fists in his pockets and watched out the window.

Eris stared for several long seconds. Trying to understand. She had never encountered someone who could not hear. The concept did not exist in the Oasis. It had never even occurred to her until she saw Diane's hands raise that gestures could be words.

Then Diane muttered, "Excuse me," and clambered past Eris over the center console to sit up in the passenger seat beside her uncle.

Eris scooted into the empty seat. Found herself missing the little points of contact: knees against knees, shoulders against shoulders. But Novak did not seem to notice. He was jiggling his knee and staring red-eyed out the window. Jaw tight.

Virgil took a sharp right, down into a basement parking garage. He killed the engine and looked at his passengers, "Okay," he said, "everybody out."

"He can talk?" Eris whispered to Novak when they got out of the car. Quietly enough that even Diane wouldn't overhear.

"Deaf people can usually talk," he

answered, patiently.

The garage was dark and nearly empty. Most of the lights had gone out, and somewhere nearby Eris could hear a faint persistent drip.

"Where are we?" she asked.

Diane told her, "Somewhere safe. Where a friend of ours lives. He wants to talk to you, really. All of us do." Fresh-sprung anxiety twisted Eris's face. Diane rushed to add, "Don't worry. We're on the same side. And we want the same thing."

Without acknowledging any of them, Virgil went over to the door marked **BUILDING UNSOUND - DO NOT ENTER**. He produced a key from his pocket and unlocked the door. A stairwell lay inside, leading up into blackness.

Eris and Novak exchanged nervous glances. Then, they followed Diane and her father up the stairs.

The haggard old building turned out to be an ancient apartment complex. Once they rose out of the basement parking, Virgil paused on the first floor to show them briefly around.

The floor was wood, the real thing, with little knots and whorls dug into its flesh. The molding on the wall had precise and intricate patterns carved into it, thick wells of dust built up inside of them. Eris ran her fingers along the little grooves in the wall, cleaning off the small flowers and thumbprint notches that reminded her of grass. In the center of the lobby sat a chandelier scattered in thousands of pieces, its metal skeleton a twisted lump on the floor.

Something moved in the hole overhead. Bats or birds. Eris did not have time to check.

Virgil was already nodding his head over his shoulder and saying, "Let me show you the way up to Rex's."

The main staircase was mostly disintegrated into a chasm with a frame. But Virgil led them to the back set at the far end of the hall. A few steps here and there were rotten all the way through, but Virgil pointed them out and warned them, softly, "Don't step there." They trailed after Virgil like a little family of ducks, following his every careful step.

At last they reached the top of the rickety stairs. The hall opened up in a wide stretch lined with apartment doors. The walls were peeling like old skin, wallpaper coming away in sheets. A waterlogged bookshelf stood against the wall, spilling swollen pages.

The building should have been dead and dark, and it nearly was.

But one door at the end of the hall had blue light seeping out from beneath the crack. The thick tail of an extension cord snaked under the apartment door and down the hall.

Virgil swung open the door and called, "Rex! I've brought you some delightful guests."

Every bone in Eris's body told her to walk back. To get out of this building with its crumbling walls and vanishing floors. But she followed Virgil toward the light, toward the man named Rex, waiting for her.

CHAPTER FIFTEEN

Eris yanked off her gas mask. The building was not airtight like newer buildings, but she couldn't deal with her sweaty scalp or the weight or the heat of it anymore.

Beyond the door was an apartment with water-swollen drywall, its wood floor covered in dust and paper and tied up bags of refuse. In the center of it all sat a desk with three huge monitors, an ancient brick of a computer, and a generator that filled the room with a low and constant hum.

The room smelled sharply of mildew and

this strange, musky scent that Eris could not quite place. Like old food and hot earth.

A man stood before the broken, boarded-up window with a glass pipe. Its bowl hot orange and smoking. Did not so much as look at them when the door opened. He pressed his lips against the spaces between the planks to blow it out.

"Come on, man," Virgil said. "Don't do that shit right now. My niece is here."

He glanced over his shoulder and grinned. "My bad," he said, the words coming out in little clouds of what was left in his lungs. He trailed a small circle with his fist over his chest: a sign, **sorry**, Eris realized a moment later.

Diane flushed dark with embarrassment. Signed something rapidly to Virgil, and his hands argued back, his face twisted with discontent.

Rex did not even seem to notice. He deposited his pipe and his lighter beside his keyboard and stood hands deep in his pants pockets. Novak stared at them long after Rex kept walking away, his face drawn.

Rex's eyes followed Eris, the light in them strange. Appraisal and fascination. All delighted calculation. "Eris Flynn," he said. "I spent all night counting my lucky stars. And now here you are."

"What?" Eris managed, feeling a little stupid.

But Rex only gave her another cryptic, unfurling smile. "You're a hard person to find, you know. And I have been trying."

Eris stared at him. He was so pale that she could see the veins running up his forearms, and his hair was dark, close-cut. He wore dark jeans, a dark sweater. Black, filthy sneakers. If not for the fat gauges in his ears and the ring pierced through his lip, he could look like anybody.

"Who are you, exactly?" Novak said.

He turned the needles of his pupils on Novak and said, "I was not talking to you."

Eris put a hand on Novak's forearm before he could react. Said for both of them, "Why were you looking for me?"

Virgil settled onto a stool by the window and watched them all, eyes darting. Eris felt as if she was excluding him just by speaking until she noticed Diane beside him, hands low but moving fast, translating subtly.

Rex glanced sideways at Virgil and then slouched down into his computer chair. "I need your help, and you need mine. I thought we could parlay."

"Parlay?" she repeated.

Novak glowered at Virgil. "Why," he asked, "did you take us to a derelict building to see a pothead?"

The man cracked a grin and caught Diane's hand gently to stop her signing. "He's more than a pothead."

"I thought you couldn't hear," Eris said, before she thought better of it. Novak patted her arm in light disapproval.

"I am among the world's shittiest lip readers," Virgil admitted, "but pothead is an easy one."

That made Eris laugh. The tension unspooled from her shoulders. Novak was still hackled as a nervous cat, but she ignored him. "What kind of help do you need from me?" she asked the man at the computer.

Now Rex eased into a smirk. He always seemed to be wearing some smile or another, each more slippery than the last. "I've been following your story, Eris Flynn. I've even found a couple of your forum accounts. But finding you yourself has been difficult. You're smart enough to use a VPN—"

"No," Novak said, "I'm smart enough to use a VPN. And I don't hear a clear answer to a simple question yet."

"It's okay." Eris reached for his hand and squeezed it.

"No, it's not. I'd like a straight answer. Because I hope you can understand why this whole situation is a bit... weird, for us."

Rex pushed himself up out of his chair and stood up to his full height. When he wasn't hunching forward, he was a few inches taller than Novak, and skinny as a blade of grass. He stopped just a few inches short of Novak and flicked his stare over him. His smile relentless and teasing now. "Oh, certainly," Rex said. "It's all very simple. I would like to help dismantle Blackwell from the bottom up. You two would like to get your friends out. And I believe we can come to an amenable agreement. Does that sound not weird enough for you?"

"Everything about you is weird," Novak muttered back, but he stepped away and looked at Eris. She saw in his eyes what he felt: he didn't like any of this, but he wouldn't tell her to leave.

Eris said, "What's your plan, exactly?"

Rex sauntered away to settle back behind

his computer. His fingers already racing across the keyboard. But even as he typed he raised his stare to survey them when he spoke. "I have invented a program that will grant any Oasis patient of my choice the access to any administrative functions. They could leave the simulation, change people's reactions, change their environment, do anything." He whirled a USB drive by its key chain. The drive itself was so thin it was nearly transparent. "But we're concerned with only one function, dear Eris."

When she just kept staring blankly back at him, Rex leaned back in his chair and folded his hands behind his head. His smile huge and sharp-edged. "No one has seen an unedited live stream of what the world is like inside of the Oasis. But the test administrators have access to it." He smirked at Eris. "We're going to give you that access."

Eris fisted her hands up in her lap. Searched Rex's eyes for the hint of a trick. "You want me to go back in there."

"Have you even *been* in the Oasis?" Novak asked, narrowing his eyes. "Do you know what you're asking for?"

"Sadly, I was not selected for that particular psychological trauma." Rex glanced over Novak, dismissively. "I was in the same lottery as the rest of you."

"So you don't know, is what you're saying."

"Why?" Eris said, ignoring both of them. Rex raised his eyebrows in an unspoken question. "Why do you need me to go in?"

"To give you evidence for your claim. To put the fire under Blackwell's ass. To make the people angry, finally." Rex folded his fingers, looking like a satisfied fox. "Those are only the primary advantages. But we need that footage. We need to see what it's like to live in the Oasis. No one is going to take you seriously otherwise."

Novak looked like he wanted to argue, but

he said nothing.

Eris glanced at the two who had brought her here. Virgil just gazed out the spaces in the boarded windows. Eyes flickering. Watching the street. And Diane met her stare, pursed her lips in a look that was all at once pleading and apology.

"Do you already have a plan?" she asked, throat creaking.

"More or less." Rex jabbed a thumb over his shoulder. "My buddy Virgil here is a janitor at Blackwell. He cleans the Oasis patients' wards at night. He just needs to pop this thing into your terminal."

"And how does she get back into the Oasis after publicly attacking it?"

"That's the genius thing. This was Virgil's idea, you should know." Rex whirled around in his chair, cupped his hands around his mouth, and shouted, "*Virgil!*" The other man glanced over at him. "I'm telling them your idea!" Rex frowned at Diane, whose hands were already moving. "Tell him I'm telling them his idea."

"Great," Virgil said, laughing.

"You just go back and lie," Rex said. "And let them think that their experiment was right after all. Let them think you miss the Oasis."

"No one would believe that after everything I've done."

"It will not take anyone at Blackwell long to realize that you are both the cause and the solution to their current media shit-storm. Your whole existence undermines their experiment, you realize that, right? Nothing could give their test better validity than you of all people recanting your statements and begging to be returned to your little cell."

For a few long moments, neither Novak nor Eris said anything.

"Can you let us think?" she ventured.

The two of them stepped out into the hall. The air seemed heavy, and Eris stood there, clutching her gas mask. The world pitched dizzily away from her like she was inside a jar slowly tumbling downhill. She was faintly aware of Novak standing in front of her, the warm wall of his presence. She wanted to fall into him. Let him just make this all go away.

But she stayed standing upright. Stayed staring at her mask in her trembling hands.

"What do you think?" he asked softly.

"I think they won't let me back out again."

"If the video is a large enough ethical controversy, they'll have to let everybody out."

"And if it isn't, I'm stuck there again." Eris did not know what she dreaded more: the administrators never letting her remember the outside world, or forcing her to crave the unquenchable taste of reality for as long as she lived in those digital walls. "And how would I get out? What if I didn't even know I was in there again? What if it's just like before?"

"I'd get you out."

"Stop it, Novak."

"You have to know I wouldn't give up. I'm not going to tell you what to choose, but you have to know that." He shook his head, stared hard at the shadowy end of the hall. "I would never just leave you in there."

Eris looked at the crack of light under Rex's door. At the bristled curve of Novak's jaw.

And she said, "I think I have to do it."

Novak didn't say anything. He just held her, fiercely, and did not let go.

CHAPTER SIXTEEN

Virgil and Diane went out to get them takeaway dinners, and soon Rex's apartment smelled like weed and sesame oil and burnt chicken. And that night, from Novak, Eris learned the names for all those scents.

Eris sat beside Novak on the patchy sagging couch. Diane settled beside her, and Virgil on a stool just over Rex's shoulder. He watched the screen and muttered corrections that made Rex occasionally roll his eyes and groan things like, "God, okay, I get that you're smarter than me."

She picked at her chow mein and tried to imagine the way that Oasis foods tasted. In the real world, food was temperature and scent and texture and flavor, and it was the feeling it left on her fingers. In the Oasis, chicken tasted more like chicken-flavored chewing gum. Horrid specter of the real thing.

Eris looked at the black-spotted ceiling, the ruined floor. Tried to hollow out this moment so she could live in it forever. The smoke and the laughter and the buzz of the generator. The realness so thick she could feel it in her very lungs.

Even Novak had lost his frayed wire edge, even as the sirens kept flaring up all over the city. He relaxed into the sofa and started showing his easy, comfortable smile again.

When night came in earnest, Virgil and Diane left. Eris gave the girl a long crushing hug before she left, murmured thank yous in her ear.

And then she was gone, down the sloping hallway. And Eris could only stand there in the doorway, hoping she would see her again.

"When do we get to leave?" Novak asked.

"You can leave whenever the fuck you want." Rex jabbed a finger at Eris. "She doesn't leave until I finish this last tweak to the program and give it another test run."

Eris frowned. "Why not?"

Rex twisted his second monitor toward her. It was a feed of recent news articles, all of them with her name. Some had pictures taken from her videos, others were still images from her protest. She had never seen her own face so full of rage.

"They are looking for you," he explained. "Enthusiastically. I don't believe you should leave until you're ready to be arrested." He paused. "Until I'm ready for you to be arrested, really."

"I won't leave without Eris," Novak said,

as if speaking to both of them.

"Honestly, I don't care what you do."

"When do you think you'll be done?" Eris asked.

"Probably by tomorrow, if I don't sleep. Definitely by the next day if I do." Rex did not even glance up from his monitors. Waved them toward the shut bedroom door. "You can take the bedroom." And then he put his headphones on and acted as if they no longer existed.

Eris and Novak did not speak much in that little room that was darkness and cool air. One of the boards over the window was loosened, and through it Eris could see the glow of the city, could hear the swishing back and forth of cars somewhere in the night. She stood with her eyes pressed to the crack, just looking out at the world.

Novak leaned his chin into her shoulder from behind. Murmured, "What are you thinking?"

She reached backwards for his arms, and he wrapped them around her. There in the cocoon of his chest she tried to remember all of this: the room full of night, the heat of Novak's breath against her ear.

"I'll miss you," she said.

"You won't have to. You'll be right back out again." He kissed the well of her collarbone. "And if you're not, I'll come in and get you myself if I have to."

Eris started laughing and weeping at the same time. She smeared hard at her cheeks and turned to bury her face in Novak's chest.

They lay that way on the bed, arms spooled around one another, whispering fears and promises, until sleep took them both at last.

***

In the morning, Rex had finished it. He showed Eris a diagnostic test she couldn't quite understand. It was just a black screen that

159

generated a series of strange bracketed words and letters that Rex pointed at delightedly and told her, "See! The little fucker finally works."

"I see," Eris said, even though she did not.

Novak peered over Eris's shoulder at the screen. "How do you know it works?" he asked.

"I stole their program data." Rex looked at Novak lazily, as if to say *obviously.* "I can't run it on this fucking thing—" he tapped his computer with his toe "—but I can at least look at their language and write something to match."

Eris didn't know what he meant, but that made Novak nod along and concede, "That is better than nothing. But how are you getting around the security protocols? I heard their IPs refresh so fast they're borderline quantum."

For once, Rex stopped looking at Novak with perfect disdain. They got deep into a discussion about third-party authenticators and the dynamic password generation system that Blackwell used. Eris could feel herself falling out of the conversation like she'd been dropped out of someone's pocket and forgotten. But eventually Novak seemed satisfied. He ran his hands through his messy hair, looked between the both of them, and said, "What's next, then?"

Rex spread his hands toward Eris. "Now Eris gets herself to Blackwell's headquarters and puts on the best show of her life."

***

To Eris's perfect surprise, Dr. Lipton did not call the police.

When she walked up to the reception desk, the receptionist stared at her for several long seconds before he lifted up the phone and said, "Please let Dr. Lipton know that her former patient Ms. Flynn would like to see her."

She felt every eye in the lobby pinned on her hotly, but she did not have to wait long. The moment he set down the phone, the receptionist stood and told her, "Right this way."

And just like that, she sat in Dr. Lipton's office in one of those huge leather chairs that made her feel so small and out of place. She ran her fingers in rapid circles over the cushion, just staring at the tiny bonsai tree on the doctor's desk.

Dr. Lipton's office was a study in minimalism. Her desk was stark, her shelves dotted only here or there by little treasures: a small exquisite statue, a succulent, a curved piece of painted glass. It felt like sitting inside an image in a magazine.

The door opened. Eris slipped her hands under her thighs to hide her restlessness.

The psychiatrist walked in, a neat and unreadable smile painted on her face. "Welcome back, Ms. Flynn."

Eris chewed hard at the inside of her lip. Said nothing. She could not spit the words out now. Not if she wanted to sound convincing. The very look on Lipton's face made Eris dizzy with anger.

Dr. Lipton relaxed into her desk chair. "You know a lot of people are looking for you right now."

"I did hear something about that."

"I have asked my staff not to call the police," the doctor explained, "out of interest in hearing your motivation."

Eris could not help her scoff.

The doctor leaned forward, her look serious and concerned. "Ms. Flynn, your behavior of late has been increasingly and very publicly erratic, paranoid, and irrational. I feel it my duty as your psychiatrist—"

"You're not my anything," Eris said through her teeth.

"I feel it my duty to offer you the opportunity to seek mental health support rather than outright turning you over to the police. Our jails are not equipped for someone like you."

"What does that mean?"

Lipton did not even flinch. "Someone paranoid to the point of borderline psychosis. You have demonstrated you lack the coping skills for this reality, Ms. Flynn."

Indignation rose like bile in her throat. Eris swallowed hard and glared at her lap, fury and embarrassment pooling hot in her cheeks. "I thought you didn't like putting words in your patients' mouths."

"I am not. I'm basing my statement off of data which you yourself have readily provided." She leaned forward, pressing her palms flat against her desk. Dr. Lipton's eyes were dark and unwavering. "I want to make sure this is perfectly clear: you run a very real risk of going to jail for the next five to ten years for inciting public violence. I am *not* your enemy here. I am trying to help you make sure that doesn't happen."

"Right," Eris muttered, her smile twisted.

"Of course you only want to help."

"I don't think you could sound more unconvinced."

Eris screwed up her jaw and glared at the little statuette on the wall behind Dr. Lipton. A woman with a rose-stem waist. Eris imagined picking it up and hurling it across the room. Watching it shatter. Then she managed, "I have something that's hard to say."

Now Dr. Lipton's look was all honey. "You can be honest with me. Better now than after you have a felony conviction, sweetie."

That *sweetie* nearly made Eris say the hell to the plan and her friends and all of it. She nearly went to jail for that word.

Instead, she shoved her rage back down and said, staring at her lap, "I want to go back. I want to go back into the Oasis."

Dr. Lipton smiled like a hungry fox.

***

Public restitution. That was Dr. Lipton's word for it.

Eris sat in her hospital gown and a pale blue robe with her script in her lap. Staring at it. Trying to wrap her mind around how a hundred little words could change everything:

My name is Eris Flynn. Two weeks ago, I chose to leave the Oasis program, and felt myself crushed with hopelessness, madness, and despair. I am so grateful that I realized my mistake. Honestly, I think the real world is too intense for people like me. I am deeply sorry for the pain and suffering my actions may have caused to anyone.

I don't know how I could go on living without the Oasis.

For all Dr. Lipton's claims that this video would be Eris's own words—her opportunity to clear her slate and make peace with the public before returning to the Oasis's electronic walls— she certainly did not mind writing this script for her.

THE CONTROL GROUP

Eris closed her eyes. Thought of Novak. Of her friends sleeping forever in rows of strangers. Never rising again, if Blackwell had their way.

She opened her mouth and began reading.

CHAPTER SEVENTEEN

Eris woke to unreality. She could feel it before she even opened her eyes.

She felt as if she was curled up in the husk of someone else's body. As if she had been reduced to a little whirring spark, watching the world from the glass walls of an enclosure. She could tell her limbs were there and functional; if she willed it, her left leg would turn and her right leg would follow, and she would stand nimbly from bed.

But she could not *feel* any of it. Her body was something she wore, not who she was. And that smallness kept her pinned to the bed until her fake mother banged on the door and called to her, "You're sleeping the day away, sweetheart!"

Eris opened her eyes. She had lived in the Oasis for over a decade, and she had never seen it like this.

Nothing had changed, but her world had become unrecognizable. The shadows cast oddly, not quite perfectly following the light of the sun streaming through the window. The quilt had no real weight on her, no feeling other than vaguely soft. When she pressed her nose to it and inhaled, she smelled nothing at all.

Outside, the trees ebbed to the same constant, gentle flow, a wind that didn't pick at the neighbors walking past on the street. The sun was high and bright and nothing like it looked in the real world, eternally eclipsed behind a thick veil of smog.

Eris pushed herself up on her elbows and rolled out of bed.

THE CONTROL GROUP

As she walked down the hall staring at family pictures she could not remember taking, it occurred to Eris that the only home she had ever known felt like a dollhouse. And she was a normal human, shrunken down, stuffed inside.

"How was your trip?" her mother asked, blinking her black buttonish eyes.

"Oh, so you're going to acknowledge my absence? That's an interesting choice."

"Sounds like somebody's sassing their mother," her father teased without looking up from his newspaper. His intonation hadn't changed in twelve years.

"I know you're not real," she told them.

Her father lowered his newspaper, his look pure and near-perfect confusion. It was uncanny to the point of being unreal. Inhuman. "What on earth are you talking about, pumpkin?"

Eris didn't bother addressing them. She wanted to rip the frying pan out of her fake mother's hand and shatter the kitchen window with it. See what those artificial fucks would do *then.*

But she took a deep breath and instead simply walked out the door, ignoring them hollering after her.

She spent all that day scouring the city for Cassius. The spot she had first found the old man was empty, his sleeping bag and makeshift tent gone. Eris had no car, and she had never been able to convince her parents to let her borrow theirs. So she walked up and down the city streets, dipping in and out of coffee shops. She even stopped strangers and asked if they'd seen an angry homeless man with a plastic bag.

If she could remember how to find it, she would just go back to Graham's place. She had only met him twice, but she remembered his kindness, the way he had treated her as if he had known her his whole life. As if simply because they understood one another, they were instant friends.

So Eris walked and walked, and it was not until twilight was gathering that she found Cassius at the little man-made pond near the center of the city. He was throwing bread at ducks and facing away from her. He still had his plastic bag full of crap, the same tight tired line to his shoulders.

For a long moment, she stood just looking at him. The city seemed to hold Cassius in the palm of its hand. He looked the way she felt: small, trapped.

"There aren't ducks in the city in the real world, you know," she called out to him.

Cassius jerked his head around and fixed her with a huge grin. At least his smile looked inevitable, natural. "You know Malia owes me fifty bucks now."

The woman's face rose in Eris's mind: huge curly hair, flashpoint rage. Eris couldn't help her own smile. "Why's that?"

"She bet you weren't coming back. And I told her she was dead fucking wrong about you." Cassius held out his arms to her, and Eris ran forward and threw her arms around him. It was like hugging a beanbag. She missed the way she could feel someone else's very blood move through them when she put her head against them.

"I told you I would."

"What the hell happened out there? What's it like?"

Eris laughed, breathlessly. "I should probably wait to tell the others."

"Nah, fuck the others." But Cassius grinned and winked and squeezed her shoulders again. "God, I can't tell you how happy I am to see you again. You got us worried, taking all that time."

"It's big, on the other side. And complicated. And..." Eris looked up at the gathering sunset. That she had never seen in the

174

real world. The sun sank like a flat red eye behind the smoke every night.

"Fine! I'll be patient." Cassius chuckled and tossed the other half of the bread loaf into the water. The ducks swarmed it. "C'mon. I'm *real* excited to see the look on Malia's face when she sees you."

A warm familiarity settled in Eris's chest as she followed Cassius up the street and listened to him babble. It felt something like home.

CHAPTER EIGHTEEN

Seeing her friends again was as elating as
it was unnerving. She did not realize until she sat
in Graham's apartment once more just how
much she had misremembered them. They were
part the people she built out of her memory and
part strangers. For example, Leo: the boy with
the hair so blond it was nearly white. She had
logged him in her memory as quiet and shy, but
tonight he seemed more edgy, intense. Unafraid
of interrupting and demanding answers directly.

Graham was the Graham she remembered.
Just as handsome, his smile just as bright and

warm. He picked her up in a rib-crushing hug and spun her in a circle the moment she walked in the door. She laughed and held him back and squealed in his ear, "Put me *down!*" in fake terror and real delight.

"You're back! I can't believe you're back! I mean, I *knew* you'd come back, but you know what I'm saying." Then Graham sashayed into the kitchen, calling something about getting her some of the iced tea he just made today. "You're going to *love* it," he told her. "It's my best batch."

"It tastes the same as all his other batches," Cassius muttered when Graham was out of earshot.

But within a few minutes of Eris walking in the door, all four of them clustered excitedly around the living room coffee table to hear her story. Even Malia's eyes, framed by sharp and perfect liner, were full of light and hope. She still wore her work clothes: filthy jeans, clunky dirt-

stained boots that she left by the door. But her
bitterness seemed to leave with her disbelief that
Eris would ever return.

"When are we getting out?" Leo blurted
before Eris could even really speak.

"I'm not sure," she admitted.

For a moment, her friends were silent,
sharing perplexed stares.

"Maybe you should just tell us what
happened," Graham finally said.

"Tell us *everything*," Malia added.

So Eris told them everything. She told
them about the outside world, with its
unbreathable air and grime-streaked cities. She
told them about Novak and all the Oasis
survivors she had met. The videos, the protests,
the runaround from Blackwell. The way Dr.
Lipton had looked at her, as if she were an
animal or an alien. How you could *feel*
everything, even the very wind moving between
your fingers. How smell was no longer just the

domain of flowers and food, with their one-note, ambiguous scents. That there was no way for a computer to recreate what it meant to smell sweetness on your fingers.

Cassius leaned back smugly in his chair. "I remember right, then."

"You left the real world when you were *seven*." Malia rolled her eyes at him. "Don't act like you're an expert. I was born there too, but I hardly remember anything but my family."

That word tore at Eris's heart. She forgot, for a moment, that Malia knew her birth family through memory. She wondered what it like to live with that kind of haunting.

"I don't know, seven years is a lot longer than a few weeks." But Cassius was smiling, and so was Malia, and for once their spat seemed good-natured.

"To be honest," Graham said, "the real world sounds kind of... shitty."

"It is kind of shitty," Eris agreed.

"And here is *massively* shitty." Leo held his hands fisted against his knees. His bright eyes burned. "When are they getting us out, Eris?"

"They... that's where it gets complicated."

Leo's look darkened into a scowl. "Why would you come back here if you didn't even have a *plan?*"

"Oh my god, is your blood sugar crashing? Why are you being an asshole? We missed Eris." Graham punched his shoulder. "Remember?"

"I'm just saying what's the point of her even getting out if she jumps right back in without doing anything?"

"I did *something*," Eris interrupted.

"I like this side of you, Leo." Malia smirked at him, somewhere between amused and impressed. "It's feisty."

Leo smiled despite himself. Blood flushed red in his cheeks and ears. "This is my sick-of-this-shit side."

"Then shut your mouth long enough for

181

Eris to tell you her idea, maybe." Cassius pulled a package of cigarettes from his breast pocket and flicked a thin white cylinder in and out, in and out. "Then if it's bad we may start building the pyre." He reached over and patted Eris's knee, as if to reassure her he was only joking.

"Blackwell won't go and release everyone. They said it would take half a year just to process *your* reevaluations. And I couldn't just wait all that time." Eris locked eyes with Leo then, who was starting to look a bit guilty for snapping. "But I met someone. He found a way to write a program that will let me access all the administrative tools within the Oasis. If we show them what it's really like in here, they'd have to let us out."

Cassius's brow dipped in confusion. "How?"

"The admins can record our perception like a video. They see and hear and feel everything we do, if they want to. Rex—the guy who made it, I mean—he said that outside of the Oasis neuro-network the sensorial patch didn't work, but it would be like a live stream video."

Now the old man settled back like a satisfied cat. "You mean they'd see everything we see? Now we'll get some real goddamn outrage brewing."

"Or they'd wonder what we're all complaining about," Malia said. She tapped her fingers against her lip. "I don't know, Eris."

"This whole place *looks* fine," Leo agreed. "If a bit... weird, at the edges."

"But we know lots of people we could interview." Graham scratched hard at the back of his head. He was clearly deep in thought, his face twisted. "Who could tell the outsiders what it's like. What it's *really* like."

"We shouldn't even tell people she's doing it." Malia stood and started pacing. Knotting up her hands in her dark coils of hair. "It has to look natural. It has to look how people really think and talk. We don't want anyone to say we're just acting."

"Oh," Graham said, "that's smart."

Malia scoffed. "You don't have to sound so surprised."

"Do it, then." Cassius leaned toward Eris, his eyes as bright and blue as a child's. "Show us how you do it."

"Do what?" Eris surveyed them all, and the hungriness in their eyes told her want they wanted. Heat rose in her cheeks. "I have to wait for the program to start. One of the people I met, um, I'm working with him. He's called Virgil. He's sneaking the program onto my unit."

"This plan is sounding increasingly convoluted," Leo muttered.

"Seriously," Malia laughed.

"I'm not hearing a single thank you out of you two," Cassius said, sounding suddenly like everybody's father. "She didn't have to come back in here for you, you know. For any of us."

Leo threw up his hands in frustration. "Well, why come back if you don't have a good plan to get out?"

"I *do* have a good plan." Eris stood and matched Leo's frown. "It's not an instant plan but it will work better than anything you've ever tried."

"There's nothing *to* try." Leo rose from the sofa and squalled into the kitchen, where he started loudly banging ice out of the tray. Graham followed him, and their heated whispers did not have to travel far for Eris to overhear.

Eris flopped down into the sofa, all her motivation leaving along with her indignation. She cupped her forehead in her palm.

Leo wasn't wrong, exactly. No one on the outside seemed to have done anything yet. She didn't feel any different. The world looked like its same flattened image, as if she was living inside a single sheet of paper. And if something had gone awry with the plan—if Virgil had been caught—if the damn drive had failed—there was no way for her to know.

"He's not usually like this," Cassius said.

"Yes, he is." Malia picked at the half-moon of dirt wedged under her thumbnail. "He's always a little bitchy."

That made the old man chuckle. "Out of all of us, he's not the bitchy one." Malia narrowed her eyes at Cassius, and he started laughing.

Eris was barely listening to them. Her mind scrambled for backup plans. She tried not to show her panic as she blurted over Malia's retort, "The psychiatrist told me you all could request to have your cases reviewed."

Malia paused and turned to frown at her. "Sorry, what?"

"The doctor. On the outside. Who helps run the test. She said you could all request an reevaluation of your involvement in the Oasis, or something."

That made Malia and Cassius both start

laughing, forgetting for a moment their own little spat.

"Girlie," Cassius said, "if that shit existed, why would we be sitting here chasing our own tails like a bunch of goddamn idiots?"

"An opt-out would affect the integrity of the experience." Malia's smile was humorless, serrated. "It would look bad for their numbers, you know."

Truth and fear and maybes rattled around Eris's skull, and for a moment she just sat there, holding her temples.

Then she raised her head and told them, "They're coming. My friends on the outside." Leo and Graham emerged from the kitchen.

Graham carried a tray of iced tea glasses and crowed, "We got drinks for everyone!" as if Leo had not just stormed out of the room.

"They're coming," she said again, looking only at Leo now. "They have to."

She tried to remember the feeling of

Novak's arms warm and heavy around her in that lovely dark. If she closed her eyes, she could almost feel the lick of his breath against her ear.

In the silence of her own heart, she told herself again and again, *he would never leave me.*

CHAPTER NINETEEN

The days ticked by and felt nearly the
same: a near-indistinguishable pile of nothing.
Every morning, no matter where she fell asleep,
Eris woke again in her own bed. As if someone
had hit a reset upon her life.

That would have been handy in the real
world. Falling asleep at Rex's and waking up in
the clean-aired cool of Novak's room.

But as the sun rose and fell over and over
in the impossible blue sky, Rex's program never
came.

She was patient. She waited. She opened

her eyes every morning to the same flat white ceiling, the same unmarred vision. She hoped to see something, a recording indicator, anything. Perhaps the program would even give her a little camera. But every day was more of the same, and each one heavier than the last.

A restlessness devoured Eris like she had never known. Every day she rose with the sun and paced up and down the length of her city, looking for secret corners, for more real humans. Every day there were more and more A.I. characters populating the houses and streets and cafes. She couldn't walk anywhere in her own city without seeing a wall of clear numbers floating over strangers' heads.

They all used the same little strips of dialogue. It seemed like half the conversations she overhead were copies of the same. And when she walked by, the fake people stared at her as if she were mythic or horrible or something in between.

But this time, Eris did not walk with her head down. She looked right through the A.I.s as if they were furniture, because they might as well have been.

She had only seen a few real people here and there. After only three weeks in the real world, Eris already found the numbers unnatural. She felt like she was living in a graveyard, surrounded eternally by the ghosts of people who had never even existed. When she saw a rare human being passing unmarked she stopped and stared and for a moment remembered that she was not alone. That she was not the strange one in all of this.

And when she found them, she went up and talked to them. Eris had never been that kind of person, the stop-and-say-hi sort. But when she peeled back the fakeness of her world, there were real people hiding underneath it. And they were worth slowing down for. They were worth talking to.

THE CONTROL GROUP

She told them who she was, what she was doing. What Blackwell intended—not just for its patients and the people on the outside, but all the billions of souls yet to be born.

Most of the people she met were tired. You could see it in the lines of their faces; they wore their own bodies like a prison.

She met a woman older even than Cassius who said that the air once looked just like the Oasis. That her grandmother once told her about growing up under a sky as wide and clear as a bowl of clean water. "It wasn't like that at all when I was a little girl, of course," she said. "My mother didn't believe in all that gas mask nonsense, and, well, the cancers got her before I was six. I always wore my gas mask after that." She chuckled, as if it was the funniest story she had ever told.

There was something else she said that stuck with Eris: "I miss the hardship the most. We have everything for nothing at all, and it means jackshit."

That Eris carried with her everywhere she went. When her fake feet became exhausted, when the simulation forced her to feel the weird tinge that was nearly hunger but more like kind of needing to shit... she just kept going. And when she ignored it long enough, it went away. Joke of a physiology. More like a missed notification on a cell phone.

"None of this is real. None of this is forever," Eris heard herself murmuring to herself over and over. It got weird, out-of-context replies from any bots who overheard her, but Eris ignored them. The mantra became the beat of her feet against the sidewalk. As the days became weeks, it was the only thing that kept her from burning her family's cozy little home down just to see if it would regenerate the next day. Cassius's hadn't, but it was worth a shot.

Something out there was real and forever. Something worth all of this.

THE CONTROL GROUP

Eris kept walking and searching and listening and waiting.

None of this is real. None of this is forever.

***

Eris's group of friends began meeting at Graham's house twice a week, just to see if Eris had any news. If anything had changed.

To everyone's credit, no one had said *I told you so* to her yet. The next time they saw each other, Leo had pulled her aside and apologized. She had held him and pretended not to notice that he'd started to weep.

She wanted to tell him that she understood. That she was scared too. But she just squeezed him back and murmured into his shoulder, "It's okay. We're okay. Everything's okay."

Eris was not sure how long she had been back in the Oasis. The count on her bedroom wall said that the weeks had become months, but she knew time passed strangely here, warped like and whetted like sunlight through a lens. She'd been gone not quite three weeks, and her friends told her it had been nine months to them. Nearly a year in only eighteen days.

Now when they met at Graham's, they spoke only of the people they had met. Whispers of Eris's plan were floating up and down the streets of the Oasis, passed among the real people in low voices, as if the A.I. would overhear.

It was a breezy Tuesday evening. Graham had the apartment windows open, and outside Eris could smell the neighbors barbecuing up something. It smelled almost real, enough to make hunger rise in her again. She had not bothered to eat, lately. There was no consequence and no point. It felt, strangely, like giving up. Like living as if the Oasis was real was the same as admitting it was.

But the cold air did not raise goosebumps along her arms. There was no sound carried on that wind, just a still silent city beyond.

Graham was babbling and waving his shish kebab around emphatically. "I met this girl the other day," he said, "who heard about Eris, and *she* said she's going to try to corrupt all the controls she can find until Blackwell has to do something."

"Right, because controls are known for being easy to find and highly receptive to the idea that their whole universe is invented." Malia rolled her eyes. Her plate was empty save for a few wooden sticks that she kept trying to stack into a strange little sculpture. "That's an unbelievably inane idea."

"Inane!" Cassius whistled. "That's a good word!"

Malia hackled. "Why do you always act like I don't know shit?"

Graham pointed his shish kebab at the both of them like a police baton and scowled. "Do we need to have another Malia and Cassius quiet hour, friends?"

"We should talk," Leo said, staring at his knees, "about what we're going to do if Eris's friends never show up."

Immediately, instinctively, Eris muttered back, "They're going to show up."

"But if they don't," Malia said, unsmiling. "Leo's right. We need a backup plan."

"What backup plan?" Cassius started laughing. "There is no backup plan."

"That's why we're talking about it, jackass," Leo said under his breath.

"If you're going to be unpleasant, at least do it loud enough so I can fuckin' hear you." Cassius rose stiffly from his chair and told Graham, "I'm getting a beer."

"That was almost asking," Graham said, which was close enough to a yes for Cassius to stomp past him to the kitchen.

Malia offered, "We could burn down the city."

That made Graham pause and scratch at his beard. "I'm trying actively to think of reasons that wouldn't work."

"What would it do other than getting us in trouble? I mean, honestly." Eris leapt to her feet and scowled around at everyone. "I fucking hate waiting like this too, but I know they won't leave us. They would never."

"They may already have," Cassius said as he swooped back into the room. He cracked his beer open loudly. "We're not talking about what you hope, Eris. We're talking worst case scenario."

"I'm telling you that scenario doesn't *exist*." For once, she felt like she needed to be the one to run off to the kitchen to calm down. She thought of Novak. The color of his eyes when he last spoke to her. He'd kissed her forehead and told her, "I'll see you again soon."

He wouldn't have said that if he didn't mean it.

But still.

The fear rooted and grew in the cracks of all the what ifs filling Eris's mind. There were so many ways for this to go wrong. So many ways that would keep Novak away from her, for months or years. Long enough for him to forget about her. Long enough to move on.

Eris slouched back into the couch and held her head in her hands. She breathed hard through her nose, trying to keep herself from crying openly.

Someone sank down onto the couch beside her. Eris looked up in time to see Leo sling his arm over her shoulder and incline his head against hers.

"We have to consider," he said, softly, "that they may have already failed."

"That would explain why we've heard

exactly shit," Malia said.

"We don't have to talk about this right now, Eris." Graham stood, probably to flutter around the room until he found the right blanket or beverage to dry Eris's tears.

"Well, we do." Cassius sounded regretful and serious. Eris did not lift her head to look at him. "We have to plan for the worst."

Eris muttered into her lap, "If it failed, then we're fucked. We're just... here. That's it."

"There's plenty we can do," Leo tried to insist, but Eris shook her head and shrugged away from him.

She stood, still hiding her face, and staggered to the bathroom. No one tried to follow her.

Eris sobbed into Graham's towel, so no one would hear her. For weeks the only thing that had dragged her out of bed every bright, unreal morning was the prayer she wore around herself like a shield: *This is not real. This is not forever.*

THE CONTROL GROUP

It would never be real, that was true. But forever hung heavy as a noose from her neck.

Eris sat on the edge of Graham's bathtub, just staring at her fingers. Waiting for the storm in her mind to pass. But as she watched the edges of her skin began to glimmer and waver, as if she was disintegrating atom by atom.

She stood unsteadily and called, "Cassius?" but when she opened her mouth the bathroom fell away from her.

She was a ghost in a perfect white world, surrounded by nothing. Full of nothing. Become nothing.

It may have been seconds or hours. She could not tell. But the downward tug of gravity pulled her down down down until the white blurred into a wall of star-speckled darkness, rushing past her so fast the specks were like streaks of light.

Eris clenched her eyes against the brightness.

And when she woke, there was the pillow under her. The blanket over her. Tickle of air traveling up her nostril, strange plastic snake wrapped around her face and ears.

Eris snapped open her eyes to stare at the ceiling of the Blackwell hospital. Tiled and freckled and real as anything. The air flushed in and out of her lungs, a feeling freshly alien and exhilarating all at once.

Her stare roved, confused, maddened. When she looked to her left she saw a familiar face standing over her.

Prim blond bun. Lip curled in a growl or a sneer or both.

Dr. Lipton's stare sank into Eris like sharpened glass. "What," she seethed, "did you *do?*"

CHAPTER TWENTY

Hope darted in Eris's belly, slippery as nausea and just as fierce.

She had done something to infuriate Dr. Lipton. That meant something had to have *worked.*

At first, Eris told the doctor nothing at all. She let Dr. Lipton stand there steaming and stewing and tugging at her blazer as the nurses helped Eris out of bed and into a wheelchair. She wanted to ask them where the kind nurse who had helped her when she first woke up had gone, but she couldn't quite remember his name. And the look on Dr. Lipton's face told her there was no room for a request.

"Take her to my office," Dr. Lipton snarled, and then she stalked out of the room, heels rapping against the tile floor.

Eris tried to insist she could walk, but the nurse patted her shoulder and reassured her, "Dr. Lipton's orders."

So she simply gripped the arms of her chair and held her breath as the nurse wheeled her down the hall. She had forgotten so much about reality even in that brief time away: the sound of distant voices, the strong stinging scent of something chemical, the feeling of her own skin wrapped over her bones. Everything was real and constant and unignorable, a wall of sensory information she had forgotten existed out here.

But there was no time to focus on that. She tried to clear her scattered scrambling mind, to figure out just what the hell Dr. Lipton meant.

Some part of the plan had to have worked. Eris held that fact between her palms like a prayer. Dr. Lipton wouldn't yank her out of the simulation in a waking phase for nothing at all.

The anger on Dr. Lipton's face had cooled like magma meeting air, dry and cracked and raging underneath. She waved the nurse away wordlessly the moment he brought Eris into the office.

For a long moment, neither of them said anything. Eris met the daggers of Dr. Lipton's stare with what she hoped looked like innocence.

Finally, Dr. Lipton spoke. "You know why I brought you here, Ms. Flynn."

"I'm afraid I don't."

Dr. Lipton slammed a little piece of plastic and metal onto her desk. Eris's belly thrilled at the sight of Rex's thumb drive, a little chunk of flexible silica with a metal tip. If Eris did not know what it was, she would have called it trash.

"Is that supposed to mean something to

me?" she asked when Dr. Lipton said nothing.

"This device was found on your console this morning. What did you *do*?" Dr. Lipton repeated, enunciating each word as if it was barbed.

"How could I put anything on your computer? I've been in a coma for I don't know how long."

"Don't play stupid with me. You stand a very real risk of going to prison for the rest of your life for tampering with federal equipment and endangering the lives of thousands of others by introducing unknown data to an extremely fragile environment."

"Then call the cops." Eris settled back into her wheelchair and folded her arms over her chest.

"Oh, don't worry, my dear. I already have." She slid the device across the table toward Eris. "But I'm giving you the opportunity to avoid my company pressing charges against you.

You only have to tell me how you got this device on your console and what its intended purpose was."

Eris stared at her knees for a long few seconds, her mind running anxious loops around itself. No one knew anything, then. It would have been all over the news. Dr. Lipton wouldn't be wasting any time demanding what the device was for if the damn thing did what it was supposed to.

Finally she said, "I can't tell you something I don't know, doctor."

Dr. Lipton slammed her fist against the table. Her voice raised to a shout. "I don't like bullshit."

"It's not bullshit. I don't even know what that *is*. I've spent all but three weeks of my life locked up in the Oasis. How would I have anything to do with whatever that is?"

"This drive was discovered on your console by one of our technicians You are the only one who could have put it there."

"Did you miss the part where I've been in an induced coma?"

"It sounds like you do want me to turn you over to the police, then."

"Yes, please. Get the police and tell them that an unconscious woman put piece of plastic crap in your stupid computer and see if they cart me off to jail. I'm happy to try it." Eris folded her arms over her chest and sat back in her chair, trying to hide the rabbiting of her heart against her ribs.

All the pieces had gone together exactly as they were supposed to, and still the plan failed. If it had worked, Dr. Lipton would be showing her hours and hours of streamed footage and demanding just how all that data got off the Oasis.

But Eris squared her shoulders and held her bluff. She would not look frightened or worried. She was blameless, as far as Dr. Lipton had to know. She only happened to be there. But behind her mind, Eris reeled, recalculating: she had to get out, find Novak, find a new plan.

Dr. Lipton sank into her chair and folded her hands to rest her chin on them. She looked at Eris as if trying to pick apart her story with her very eyes. "I don't believe you for a second," Dr. Lipton told her.

"You don't have to. But I think we both know you have no proof of anything."

The doctor plucked up the little drive between her fingernails and gave it a belittling smile. "I may not know what you meant to do with this little toy, Ms. Flynn, I can assure you it did not work. All our systems are operational. Our security system remains unimpacted. You can be coy and smug all you want, but there is something else both of us know: whatever you tried to do, you failed."

Eris opened her mouth to argue, but the secretary peeped over the intercom, "Uh, Dr.

Lipton?"

Dr. Lipton held down the intercom button. "Not now," she snapped back.

"This is sort of an emergency."

She snatched the phone up and roared, "*What?*" into the receiver. Then, for a long few moments, Dr. Lipton sat listening. She pivoted around in her desk chair to face her exquisite shelves and knickknacks. And as Eris watched, the doctor's shoulders crumbled forward as she leaned forward to clutch her forehead.

"You're fucking kidding me," she murmured after several long silent minutes.

Dr. Lipton slammed the phone down so hard the plastic base cracked. She raised her livid stare to Eris. She looked as if she wanted to lean over the table and slap Eris across the mouth.

Oh, Eris thought, biting back her grin. *It definitely worked.*

CHAPTER TWENTY-ONE

This time, Dr. Lipton did call the police.

They showed up within ten minutes of the video going live. Dr. Lipton stalked around her office like an enraged lion. She would not look at Eris. Would not look at anything but her phone, which kept playing the video over and over again. Dr. Lipton put in tiny wireless earbuds so that Eris would not overhear, but Eris didn't need to.

She knew by the look on Dr. Lipton's face what was on that phone.

When the police came, they handcuffed Eris to her chair, helped her ease on a gas mask, and wheeled her out the front doors of Blackwell's test facility.

The parking lot outside was already half-full of media vans, and more still poured into the parking lot in a long caravan. Some of the vans at the end of the line had people spilling out with cameras and lights and boom mics to rush around the traffic. The reporters and their cameras crowded at the steps of the hospital, murmuring amongst themselves.

When the doors peeled open, the questions hit Eris as a wave of sound. She blinked and stared, wishing this was a full-face mask. Wishing she could hide her shock and fear behind the glass walls of eye covers.

But the cameras caught her confusion. The reporters demanded,

"Ms. Flynn! How did you do it?"

"Who were those people inside the Oasis? Are those real patients?"

"Can you tell us what it's like in there? Ms.

Flynn!"

Eris clung to the arms of her wheelchair. Suddenly, she felt grateful for the police. She could not imagine leaving this building by herself.

The officers helped her stand up and shuffle into the car, legs stringy and weak after so many days of wakeless sleep.

**

Eris did not watch the video go up. She had been sitting across the desk from Dr. Lipton and doing her best to look faultless. No one could reasonably make the argument that she had done it.

But still she sat in that interrogation room, hands folded in her lap. They had gotten her a change of clothes, an ill-fitting Seattle PD sweater and a huge pair of sweatpants. She had to fold the band over thrice just to keep the ends of the pants from dragging on the ground.

A detective sat across the table from her with a tablet in his hands. He glanced at her over the rim of his glasses.

"Are you aware of why you've been brought here today, Ms. Flynn?"

"I heard something about a video?" Eris cleared her dry throat. Sipped the water the detective had brought her. "I'm not sure. It was all very confusing."

"Would you like to see what you've been accused of?"

Eris could not tell from this man's face if he thought she was innocent or guilty. She only offered a silent nod and hoped she looked more confused than elated.

The detective slid the tablet across the table to her. It was a ten minute video, and the moment it started Eris recognized it. Recognized everything.

It was her first day back inside the Oasis.

THE CONTROL GROUP

Here in this real room, with its harsh incandescent lights and its real lingering shadows, everything in her room looked so... fake. Like parts of a video game. Even the way her family moved and looked at her was just strange enough at the edges to make Eris's belly turn with a familiar horror.

She heard herself snap at her fake father, "I know you're not real." And his senseless, maddening reply.

She saw all the people she had met, their lives captured in little thirty second bursts played one after the next.

Tears gathered thick and hot in Eris's throat as she realized: it had worked all the while. Rex had watched it all, picked out the finest little gems of Eris's memory, and put them here for the world to see. All that fear and worry for nothing and everything. She didn't know if she wanted to sob or laugh.

"How did they get this?" she managed

when the video ended. "Did... that was inside my head. How could someone take it?"

The detective set Rex's little thumb drive on the table. "Have you seen this device before?" he asked.

"Dr. Lipton had it. She said it was on my machine. I tried to tell her I have no idea. I don't even know how computers work, really." Eris shoved her hands under her thighs. Her eyes felt glassy and huge, and she hoped it would make the detective feel sorry for her. "Did... do you think someone hacked *me?*"

That made the detective laugh. The tension eased out of his shoulders. "It doesn't *quite* work that way, but that is basically our working theory, at the moment." He took the tablet back and regarded Eris with a light smile. "I feel confident in saying that we don't consider you a person of interest at this time, Ms. Flynn. You have an extremely solid alibi, and the encryption on this device suggests that our suspect is no amateur. This is a formality, at this point." The detective tapped at the tablet and brought up another screen. A white document full of lines and boxes. "I will have to ask you to tell me everything you remember."

Eris did, more or less. She told him about waking up baffled and terrified. The way that Dr. Lipton had accused her. How she had just sat there, bewildered, until the police came and brought her here.

"To be honest," Eris finished with a shaky laugh, "I have no idea why I'm even wrapped up in all this. It feels like a sick joke."

The detective finished typing up notes on his tablet and shut it off. He folded up his hands and frowned at Eris. "Ms. Flynn, I am afraid I must tell you that you have been barred from all Blackwell property. Your doctor has secured an immediate emergency restraining order against you."

"I am in trouble?" she asked.

"No, not legally, or judicially. As far as I'm aware. But this little thing—" he held up the drive "—has done quite a lot to destroy Blackwell's credibility in only a few hours. I'm not surprised that they'd rather you stay away from their facilities in the future." He offered her a wink.

Eris put her hands over her mouth to hide her smile. "But the Oasis is all I've ever known," she said.

The detective chuckled and gestured to his tablet. "It looks like you're not missing out on very much, to be quite honest with you." He stood up and walked around to Eris's side of the table to offer her his hand. "Well, those are all the questions I have for you. I'd be happy to escort you out, if you need it."

She almost declined. But when Eris stood up and felt the ache in her muscles, she accepted the detective's hand gratefully. She clutched his arm and limped down the hall.

Eris wanted to ask what his name was. If he knew anyone in the Oasis. If he knew that anyone else was getting out. But she just clung to him wordlessly and tried not to lean into him too much.

When they reached the end of the hall, the detective stopped at the heavy double doors. The glass was reinforced with steel wire, and through it Eris could see the waiting room beyond.

"This is where I stop," he told her, giving her elbow a reassuring squeeze. "Will you be alright from here?"

Eris loved him more in that second than she had ever loved her Oasis-father. Perhaps if the Oasis programmers had thought to include better affection, she never would have tried to leave. Never would have met Novak. Perhaps none of this would have ever happened.

She didn't tell him any of that. She only smiled and nodded. "Thank you," she said. "For everything."

The detective laughed. "I didn't do a damn thing." He held open the door for Eris and nodded at the waiting room. "Your friend is here to pick you up."

Her throat constricted. Eris limped past him to see Novak standing there, looking out the window. His back was to her, but she would recognize him anywhere.

She leaned against the wall and said, "Hey there."

Novak turned. His face split in relief and warmth and longing. He hurried across the room and threw both arms around her. Held her tight and fierce, as if he never wanted to let go.

"You have no idea how much I missed you," he murmured in her ear.

And finally, Eris let herself cry.

CHAPTER TWENTY-TWO

The uproar was immediate and everywhere. Within forty-eight hours of the video going up, the media and internet combined had raised absolute hell in Eris's name.

Eris spent those two days holed up in Novak's apartment. She had only tried to go out once, the first day after she got out. It was supposed to be a quick, quiet trip to the grocery store, but someone must have recognized them. She felt eyes following her everywhere she went.

And when they emerged, the parking lot already had three or four television crews huddled around the front door. The moment Eris stepped out, still trying to click her gas mask into place, they bombarded her with question after question.

"What is the real world like compared to the Oasis? Is it better out here? Is it really as bad in there as the video makes it seem?"

Eris had just stood there, frozen, while Novak smacked the nearest boom mic and told them all, "Yeah, no thanks," which was his way of saying *fuck off.*

She had never anticipated becoming a celebrity. But no one on television could talk about Blackwell without linking her name to it.

Eris Flynn, the symbol of everything wrong with the Oasis. Eris Flynn, the reason we could not stand for any of this any longer.

Eris barely knew what it meant to be herself anymore. Everything seemed strange and impossible now. She saw pictures of herself she had never seen before everywhere: on television, on the computer. The day she went out, an ethics league had even installed a billboard with her face on it, urging passersby LISTEN TO THE SURVIVORS.

But Eris felt most like herself in the quiet moments when she and Novak were alone and reading or cooking or kissing (god, they had done so much *kissing*, and Eris had never craved a feeling more) or when he ran his fingers gently through her hair as they talked in whisper-quiet on the edge of sleep.

On the third day of her life in the real world, Eris woke to Novak shaking her awake, urgently. She had slept in Novak's bed every night since she came home, folded up in the comfortable well of his arms.

"What?" she asked, sleepily.

"We have to go to the hospital. Right now."

"What? Are you okay?"

"Of course I am."

Eris blinked the sleep out of her eyes and saw that he was grinning. "What happened?" she said.

"They're letting them out. Everyone."

"From Oasis?"

"They shut the fucking thing down, Eris. They're shutting it all down." He gripped his wild hair with both hands adorably.

Eris couldn't help her smile. "We did it?" she asked.

"You did it. I'm just here for looking good and moral support." Novak grinned and picked her up out of bed, spun her in a circle as she squealed. He set her down, put his hands on her cheeks, and kissed her. "Come on! We need to go!"

Eris stumbled into a clean pair of pants and followed Novak out the door.

She did not care that she was recognized. She barely even slowed enough to put on her gas mask. When people asked her, "Are you that

Oasis girl?" she nodded back and just kept walking.

There was no more reason to be afraid of who she was. She was in the right, after all this time. She had won.

First, Novak took them to Rex's. The derelict building seemed warm and comforting to her now, like a friendly ghost she had forgotten was waiting for her. Novak led the way up with new practiced ease, picking his way nimbly over the broken steps. He gripped her elbow the whole way, refusing to let her go it alone.

"You're still recovering," he reminded her. "Let me help you."

"But—" she tried.

Novak gave her a dewy smile. "I love helping you." And that was enough to make Eris relent.

"How do you know this place so well?" she asked.

They paused at the top of the stairs. Novak smiled shyly at his feet as Eris leaned into him. She did not need that much help to stand up, not really. But she liked the closeness. The feeling of her body against his.

"You were in there only another ten days," he said. "I think Rex did nothing but watch your neural stream for, like, two hundred hours that week. But I came here every day, just to check up on you."

Relief pooled warm in Eris's belly. It had worked from the start. That fact would never stop amazing her. Her smile was like wire unspooling. "You know that's adorable."

"Oh, hush." He pecked a kiss to the top of her head and walked with her to Rex's door.

Virgil and his niece Diane were already there, crowded around Rex's computer. When Novak swung the door open, Rex clapped his hands over his head in a slow, constant applause.

"The star of the show!" he crowed.

Diane leapt over to give Eris a crushing hug. "You did it! You're here!"

"I did!" Eris agreed, breathless and elated. She clutched Diane's arms for support. "Why is everyone here?" she asked. She panned her stare around the room: Rex, smug and grinning, spinning a lighter between his fingers. Virgil, who looked happy just to see Diane happy.

When Virgil caught Eris's eye he waved and said, "Well done. You gave us more footage than we knew what to do with."

"I couldn't have done it without you. Any of you."

"Well, fucking duh." But Rex's smile was huge and delighted, like a child's. "Come on, Eris Flynn. You've finally given me a reason to go outside." He stood up from his desk and patted Eris's shoulder as he passed her for the gas mask hanging from the wall by a nail.

"And what's that?" she asked, laughing.

Another easy smirk. "It's time to go get

your friends."

***

Within an hour, the four of them arrived at the swollen parking lot outside of Blackwell's hospital. Cars crowded every spare inch the parking lot. A line of vehicles stretching a mile down the road waited just to get into the lot.

Eris clung to Novak's elbow and tried to halfway hide behind him. There were little hordes of newspeople everywhere, trying to immortalize this moment. Eris prayed none of them would notice her. This story was bigger than her, after all; it was all the thousands of people waking up to find themselves finally free, for better or for worse.

She wondered at the other controls. What they must be feeling right now. To wake suddenly in a world that was not their own. A world they never even knew existed.

THE CONTROL GROUP

"I think your support group is going to get a lot more crowded," she muttered to Novak. His laugh humming through his chest calmed and grounded her. She leaned her ear against his ribs just to hear it better.

It was complete madness. Bleary-eyed people in hospital gowns or clothes they hadn't worn in decades poured out of the hospital. Most of them could not walk, and Eris knew herself what a process it was to teach her muscles how to support her body all over again.

But she waited patiently outside with the rest of them, bounced up on her toes. Watching. Waiting.

Most of the people who came out had disposable gas masks, flimsy plastic things that only covered one's face and mouth and had to be thrown out after a few hours. But it was enough to get them out the door and to some semblance of home.

Finally, she recognized someone. Leo. He

was curled up small like a child, gripping his wheelchair with his thin, birdlike arms. An attendant wheeled him out and boomed through a megaphone, "Leo Klein. Is anyone here for Leo Klein!"

Eris stepped forward and threw her hand up in the air.

She couldn't see his mouth, but she could tell by his eyes that Leo was beaming at her. He smeared hard at the tears that chased down his cheeks.

Eris ran forward and held him so tightly she nearly lifted him out of his seat. She was exhausted, her balance pitching, but he held her back like she was everything.

"Come on," she told him. "Let's wait for the others."

One by one, the rest of Eris's friends trickled out. Cassius looked younger in the real world than he ever had in the Oasis. He wore time differently out here; perhaps it was the lack of sunlight that did it, or that his real, unconscious body had never smiled enough to form the wrinkles she knew so well. But when he caught sight of Eris, his familiar smile returned, instantly, and folded up the skin around his eyes.

Graham emerged on crutches. An orderly hovered nearby, nervously, but Graham waved her away and insisted, "I'm fine! See? I'm walking. I'm fine." His smile was tight and tired, but it only grew bigger when Leo yanked down his gas mask to yell, "Graham! Over here! Graham!"

Graham staggered over to them and hugged Leo first. Tore off his gas mask just to pepper the boy's forehead with kisses. Then he introduced himself to all of Eris's real world friends. Graham was just as animated and social as he had been inside the Oasis, happy as a puppy to meet everyone. He even got Rex to admit that he had made the program and got Rex babbling about encryption and how he hid the data packets in the Oasis's regular upload traffic.

Virgil muttered low to Diane, "I've never been so happy I don't have to listen to him," and the girl hid her giggle in her palms.

The last to emerge was Malia. Her hair was in a limp bun, and her face seemed strangely bare without her eyeliner. But she was herself, just as real as the air and the skeletons of trees. But when the attendant called out her name, Eris was not the first one to speak.

A woman with hair just as thick and curly pushed her way through the crowd. She wrenched off her gas mask, raised her hand high over her head, and called to anyone who would listen, "That's my daughter! That's my daughter!"

Malia started sobbing the moment her mother broke through the crowd. She didn't even see Eris. She just held her mother and cried. And then when the nurse lightly touched her mother's shoulder, the woman wheeled Malia away from the doors.

As they passed by, Malia caught Eris's eye. She smiled and pulled the mask away from her mouth long enough to mouth the word *thanks*.

Eris nodded and beamed but she did not try to stop her.

Then she turned to face her friends. Real and physical and perhaps not altogether well, but whole. And here.

Novak took her hand and held it, tightly. "Well," he said, "I guess we'd better find you all some better gas masks."

That won a laugh out of everybody. They turned and walked down the road together, back toward the train station.

The sun hung low in the sky, a pale red disc behind the clouds. Eris turned her face up to watch it watching over them.

Everything was beautiful, she thought, even if it hurt.

EPILOGUE

Soon, reality felt like the only thing Eris had ever known.

She was stronger than she ever had been. Her legs no longer shuddered from a simple walk to the store and back again.

In the mornings she would walk down to the gym near her apartment. The first day she had gone in, the gym owner had held her and wept and thanked her for returning her son. "I surrendered him during the famine," she explained as she wiped away her tears. "I never thought I would see him again." And ever since, she insisted Eris come use the facility for free. Every time Eris came in the owner stopped to ask her about Novak and all the Oasis survivors.

And Eris would always smile, shyly, and tell her, "They're great. It's great. Honestly, everything is better than I could have imagined."

And it was. The city was more crowded, true, and Novak's support meetings had become so full of people he held them nearly every night with a different crowd. Eris went with him most of the time, part to help, and part just to be near him.

She walked back from the gym that morning with her heart full of light. Lately she wore Novak's gas mask, even though it was almost too big for her, because it was large enough to stuff her hair under the cap. She preferred slipping by unrecognized, but she could always tell another Oasis survivor, because they recognized her almost immediately.

When she met someone from out of the

Oasis, she always stopped to hear their story. There was never a moment too busy for Eris, not anymore. Most of the stories people told her were positive: lovers and mothers and fathers and children and siblings brought together again after decades of distance. Once in a while, she met someone infuriated with her for pulling them out of the Oasis for *this*.

And when she met those people, Eris just smiled up at the smog all around them and said, "Yes. I think it's all worth it, in the end."

Today, on her walk back from the gym, she recognized no one. She was relieved to pass like a ghost through her familiar city streets. As she walked, she ticked her eyes over every face she passed. It was comforting to look at everyone and know they were just as human as she was.

Eris walked up the steps of her home. Let herself into her and Novak's apartment. She remembered when it had just been his, when she had felt like a strange and irritating guest. But now this home felt as much hers as his. She had rescued an old oil painting from a thrift store and hung it up in their living room. They cooked and washed up together every evening. They talked, constantly, and Eris could not hear his voice often enough. She wanted to fill herself up with his every word.

She shut the door and pulled off her gas mask with a weary sigh.

Novak was in the kitchen, whipping up breakfast. It filled the room with a heavenly scent. "You know your old gang is going to group tonight. Graham told me."

"Well, that's a relief." Eris stuck the gas mask on the hook by the door. Hung up her coat alongside it. "Although I think Cassius will fill up the whole two hours bitching about the two of them."

Leo, Graham, and Cassius had a shared apartment on the other side of the city. An old tenement building that had been hastily renovated to be livable. Blackwell's court order—which had been agreed upon to keep most of Blackwell's executives out of prison for intentionally obfuscating data and misleading the public—had involved securing housing and medical care for all its former patients for the first year after their release from the program.

Eris remembered when that was still being hotly debated on television. She had released a brief video demanding proper restitution for Blackwell victims. Novak had written the best line in the whole damn thing: "You stole our lives from us; now you owe us the chance to start over again."

That made Novak laugh. He nodded over to the oven. "Come help me, lady."

Eris swished into the kitchen to stir the eggs before they could burn. She knew Novak did not really need her help to keep sausage and eggs from burning, but he took the opportunity to loop his free arm around her middle.

"I'm sweaty," she told him, laughing.

"I don't care."

They stood together before the stove. Eris pillowed her head against his shoulder and listened to the oil sizzle and pop in the pan.

"Do you ever miss it?" she asked him.

"Hmm?"

"The Oasis."

Novak paused. He poked at the sausage links thoughtfully. "I suppose I miss some things. I miss clean air."

Eris laughed. "Well, sure."

"What about you?"

She beamed up at him. "Not for a second."

He laughed. "Well, it was beautiful in there. Even if it did feel like a video game." He smiled and held her closer. "But you make reality a good deal prettier."

"Oh, stop it, you fuckin' cheeseball." But Eris was blushing and grinning and turned her face up to meet Novak's kiss. She had never kissed anyone in the Oasis, but surely it could not feel this good.

Novak flicked off the heat to the stove. Pressed her against the counter. Kept kissing her. She savored the taste of him.

"The food's going to—" she started, but Novak just murmured, "Shh," against her lips and pulled her toward the bedroom.

Their food was cold by the time they came back into the kitchen to eat breakfast.

It was the best thing she'd ever tasted.

E.C. Static is a pen name, but the author has been writing for over a decade. She holds her bachelor's degrees in English literature and psychology. And she's tired of talking in the third person, so...

If you enjoy my writing, you can read more (for free!) at:

www.reddit.com/r/shoringupfragments

70964490R00146

Made in the USA
Middletown, DE
19 April 2018